ALSO BY ELIZABETH McCRACKEN

Here's Your Hat What's Your Hurry

The Giant's House

Niagara Falls All Over Again

Exact Replica of a Figment of My Imagination

Thunderstruck and Other Stories

Bowlaway

The Souvenir Museum

An E

The Hero of This Book

A NOVEL

Elizabeth McCracken

An Imprint of HarperCollins*Publishers*

This is a work of fiction. Names, characters, places, and incidents are products of the author's imagination or are used fictitiously and are not to be construed as real. Any resemblance to actual events, locales, organizations, or persons, living or dead, is entirely coincidental.

The author would like to thank United States Artists for a fellowship that made all the difference in the writing of this book.

THE HERO OF THIS BOOK. Copyright © 2022 by Elizabeth McCracken. All rights reserved. Printed in the United States of America. No part of this book may be used or reproduced in any manner whatsoever without written permission except in the case of brief quotations embodied in critical articles and reviews. For information, address HarperCollins Publishers, 195 Broadway, New York, NY 10007.

HarperCollins books may be purchased for educational, business, or sales promotional use. For information, please email the Special Markets Department at SPsales@harpercollins.com.

Ecco® and HarperCollins® are trademarks of HarperCollins Publishers.

Photograph on dedication page courtesy of Matt Valentine.

Excerpt from "In the Waiting Room" from POEMS by Elizabeth Bishop. Copyright © 2011 by The Alice H. Methfessel Trust. Publisher's Note and compilation copyright © 2011 by Farrar, Straus and Giroux. Reprinted by permission of Farrar, Straus and Giroux. All Rights Reserved.

FIRST EDITION

Designed by Paula Russell Szafranski

Library of Congress Cataloging-in-Publication Data has been applied for.

ISBN 978-0-06-297127-2

22 23 24 25 26   LSC   10 9 8 7 6 5 4 3 2 1

Here's
Your Hat
What's
Your
Hurry

For Mom—
—whose life history I will
continue to mine, but who will
never — no matter what she
or anybody else thinks—
appear as a character in my
work, being too good for the
likes of me & my characters.

love
Elizabeth

Mother's Day
1993

But I felt: you are an *I*,

you are an *Elizabeth*,

you are one of *them*.

Why should you be one, too?

—from
"In the Waiting Room,"
Elizabeth Bishop

The
Hero
of This
Book

This was the summer before the world stopped. We thought it was pretty bad, though in retrospect there was joy to be found. Aboveground monsters were everywhere, with terrible hair and red neckties. The monsters weren't in control of their powers—the hate crimes, mass shootings, heat waves, stupidity, certainty, flash floods, wildfires—but they had reach. *Everyone talks about the weather, but nobody does anything about it.* Turns out we were supposed to.

August 2019: I shouldn't be vague, though that's my nature. Things felt dire, which now seems laughable. You could still unthinkingly go places. Myself, I'd gone to London, where a heat wave had bent train rails and shut down art exhibitions and turned the English into pink, panting mammals. I, pink, mammalian, panted alongside them. I was trying to decide what I thought about my life.

On the internet I'd found a small hotel in Clerkenwell, a neighborhood I hadn't heard of. "*Clark*enwell," the owner of the hotel clarified when I arrived, but I couldn't get the hang of deforming only the one *e* and kept calling it Clarkenwall. He was a gentle, blinky Englishman named Trevor, who might have been thirty and might have been fifty. He had a shaved head, hoops in both ears; he wore espadrilles, long loose shorts, and a brown linen vest, which he surely called a waistcoat and surely pronounced *weskit*. Altogether he looked like someone who was either a vegan or knew how to mindfully butcher a pig and use up every bit, snout and kidneys, trotters and tail.

Perhaps you fear writing a memoir, reasonably. Invent a single man and call your book a novel. The freedom one fictional man grants you is immeasurable.

"Here for pleasure?" Trevor asked. "Or is it work?"

"Bit of both," I said finally, with an accidental English accent.

Trevor smiled. His canines were obelisks. "Come this way. You'll like it here. Full of history. They used to hang people on the green."

"Wonderful," I answered.

The usual feeling of having my fortune told came over me, as it did whenever I approached accommodation for the first time. Good, I was blessed; bad, cursed. A short list of my minor obsessions: hotel rooms, fortune-tellers, coin-op machines. Embarrassing, how much I refer to fortune-telling in my life—by *life*, I mean writing. Not memoir: I am not a memoirist. The room at Trevor's was on the ground floor—a curse—but the photos on the website hadn't done justice to the green leather armchair or shown at all the little desk in the bay window, the old cast-iron stove set into the fireplace.

Trevor's hand, as he gestured, was knuckly and atremble. "Cooker's original to the house," he said. "Georgian. There would have been a whole family in this one room. Just the two nights?"

"Yes," I said, "alas." *Alas* was one of those things I said too often, a way to say no while presenting myself as helpless.

He nodded. His eyes, like the chair, were oddly green. "I'll leave you to it."

The bathroom had a snub-nosed slipper tub and a toilet that flushed with a pull chain. At the bottom of the toilet bowl in pale-blue letters baked into the porcelain were the words *Thomas Crapper—London, Ltd*. Such a world, that has such toilets in it!

I put my laptop on the desk in the window and drew the curtains, to reveal another pair of curtains, and drew those curtains to reveal a sheer panel attached at both top and bottom. There were pubs on either side of Trevor's place. I could hear the drinking Londoners on the street: conversation, blunt laughter. Two men moved in front of the window like burly shadow puppets, inches away from me. I could see their shapes but not details. "Tenerife's no good," one said to the other, bringing his pint glass to his mouth. "Tenerife's where I fucked up." I switched on the desk lamp, its glass shade the same Robin Hood green as the armchair. Peter Pan green. Poison green. If the drinkers had noticed me, I would have looked to them like an automatic fortune-teller in a box. *Go back to Tenerife,* I thought at the man outside, *and find your true love.* Perhaps I'd write this advice on the back of a business card and push it through a crack at the bottom of the window.

Never give up your metaphoric bad habits, the way your obsessions make themselves visible in your words. Tell yourself that one day a scholar will write a paper on them, an x-ray of your psyche, with all of your quirks visible like breaks in bones, both healed and fresh.

I took out the burner phone I owned for international travel, turned it off, and set it on my desk so that I wouldn't be woken up by a middle-of-the-night text from America. The one person who might need me, the simmering emergency and joy of the past few years, my mother, was ten months dead. The last time I'd been to London was with her in 2016, after the presidential election but before the inauguration, on a lark of a Christmas trip. We'd had an exceptionally good time. I'd only minimally sniped at her. I'd let her make every decision and I'd picked up every check.

Condoling friends used the words *grief* and *mourning*. But neither was what I felt. All my life I'd heard people use those words to discuss the ordinary deaths of elderly people—or, worse, elderly animals—and (I am hard-hearted) I found them melodramatic. Those old people and dogs were never going to be immortal. Grief, as I understood it—grief and I were acquainted—is the kind of loss that sets you on fire as you struggle to put it out. My mother's death hadn't changed my mind. I just missed her. I hated to see her go. But she'd had a sweet end, or so I kept telling people, though who was I to speak for my mother? She'd hate that, my opinion about her experience. It was sweet for her family, at home with hospice nurses and cats, and friends around the bed, at a time—2018—when you couldn't count on a sweet end but it wasn't impossible.

At my Clerkenwell (*Clark*enwall, *Clark*en*well*) desk, I read an email from the real estate agent who was going to try to sell my mother's house in far-off Massachusetts. A crew of professionals had cleaned it, organized the contents, held an estate sale, and then swept all the leftover things into three dumpsters. The estate sale I had attended; the clean-out, as it was called, happened afterward, over weeks, though I hadn't seen the pictures or heard how much the sale had netted. The real estate agent had grown up in the same Italian American neighborhood as I had (I was not Italian American), with the same sort of name as the boys from my elementary school, which is why I had picked him, though he was ten years older than me and my former classmates, a youngish senior citizen in a blue suit. I didn't know him, a relief. One of my mother's neighbors was keen to sell the house for me, had in fact met my mother while canvassing the street for houses to sell, had in fact emailed me to offer condolences and her services. I was tired of people who'd known my mother getting in touch with me, not because they had no claim but because they did. In London, I found I wanted to hoard my little portion of her. I didn't write back to the neighbor, or to the Russian handyman who worked for my mother and wanted to know whether he should cut the lawn, or to his wife, an enthusiastic though incompetent house cleaner who brought my mother homemade chopped liver and loved her entirely. Mow the lawn? It was a reasonable question. I just didn't want to answer it. I didn't even write back to the real estate agent, whose daughter, he said, had taken pictures of the house: The listing would be up by the end of the American day. Let him list the house. Let it disappear without me noticing. It wasn't a haunted house but a haunting one. It had haunted me a long time.

Bereaved. That I'd own up to. *Bereaved* suggests the shadow of the missing one, while *grief* insists you're all alone. In London, I was bereaved and haunted.

The house was for sale. Soon I would have nothing to do with it.

I didn't want to see the pictures. I didn't want to work,

either. I closed my laptop and felt the internet burble through the lid, felt it flow into my fingers and hectic wrists. The next day, I decided abruptly, I would spend the whole day out, just my internetless burner phone in my pocket. I would let the city fill my head, and I would be a person on the earth instead of on the internet. I loved the internet, no mistake—the natter, the burble, the possibility of offered love, the opportunity to ask for love and receive it, never unalloyed, perhaps only fool's love, shining like the real thing, which was sometimes good enough even if it didn't last so long. The thrill of finding fool's love was still a thrill. The internet, or my relationship to it, had become a sixth sense, a shitty one, a power I used to divine things, sure, but also a prickling sensation in my organs: *There is information out there, better find it!* The monsters, too, whose power lived in the way they convinced you that you could defeat them with words they'd never read. I had a fantasy that someday I would meet one or two of these monsters, shake a hand, lean forward, and whisper the one thing each would most hate to hear. *You do know you're going to hell. Fat ass. Everyone can tell how stupid you are. God doesn't love you. Your wife doesn't love you. Your children will forget you. You're going to hell. You're going to hell. You're going to hell.*

As for myself, I didn't believe in hell or an afterworld of any sort. What netherworld could be more nether than this one? I believed the afterlife was, as an atheist might tell a child curious about heaven, the memories of other people. How my mother would have hated that! To cede control to other people's brains, when her own brain was what she trusted. Still, she loved being thought about.

"You know," said the man on the other side of my window, the one who'd fucked up in Tenerife, "that's how it is. Do you know what I mean?"

"Yeah."

"But do you know what I *mean*?"

My mother distrusted memoirs and I wasn't interested in the autobiographical and for a long time that made things easy. But writers change even if mothers don't.

(Mothers change plenty. Don't trust a writer who gives out advice. Writers are suckers for pretty turns of phrase with only the ring of truth.)

Everything makes more sense if you know what my parents looked like. My father was six foot three and, for the last forty years of his life, enormous in every dimension, three hundred pounds or more. Photos reveal that he was relatively thin for parts of my early childhood. That father, the one with a mustache and plenty of sandy-blond hair, has been replaced in my head by the white-bearded fat father, the one children on the street mistook for Santa Claus, which he enjoyed as long as a nearby parent didn't say, "You better be good, or he won't bring you any presents!" He was mostly shy. Some people were frightened by his size and silence; in my childhood I sometimes was. He had a stutter and a temper and an encyclopedic memory, a capacious metaphorical heart and an enlarged anatomical one. He didn't take care of himself. His eyes were large and very blue. You couldn't tell exactly how many teeth he'd lost to neglect (I don't remember him ever going to a dentist) because his beard hid it. My mother was less than five feet tall, walked with canes during my childhood, had tarnished black hair she wore in a bun, was talkative, had black eyebrows even when her hair had gone mostly white, was olive-skinned (she said that wherever she went, she met lonely men who mistook her for a countrywoman, spoke Turkish and Spanish and Urdu at her; once, in print—in *The New Yorker*—a famous friend of my father's described a dinner with my parents, a "Rabelaisian prodigy" and "his wife, a beautiful Oriental"). She was a Jewish girl of Eastern European descent, born in a small town near Des Moines, Iowa, the older of twin girls. She always loved what made her statistically unusual.

I have no interest in ordinary people, having met so few of them in my life.

Any writer will be asked, *Why?* Why write; why write *this* book; what made you do it. If I showed you a photograph of my parents, I think you'd understand.

They met in Des Moines, at Drake University, then moved from one institution of higher learning to another. My mother got her doctorate at the University of Wisconsin–Madison; my father would have but never finished his dissertation. They both taught for a while but eventually ended up at Boston University on staff. We lived in the nearest western suburb.

After my father's death, the house became *my mother's house;* after her death, *my parents' house* again. I don't know when it stopped being *my house,* though I lived there for fourteen years, from second grade till I graduated college. Once I moved away, I disowned the house; I worried about it. The place was a firetrap, crammed with stacks of paper, with Jazz Age wiring and addlepated appliances. I tried not to think about it, but I failed. The house might catch fire and burn to the ground. The fire might sweep through the neighborhood. Some municipal official in my hometown (though I never thought of that suburb as *my hometown*) might call to blame me. The head of the Board of Health. ("If I don't bathe, I'm going to be condemned by the Board of Health," my mother sometimes said.) Maybe the mayor would call me up. When I was a kid, the mayor was an exuberant man who, like my mother, was Jewish and dusky, who favored pale suits, and even now when I hear of a generic mayor it's him that I see. *Kid,* he'd say. *How could you have let this happen? How could you have allowed your elderly parents to live in this shithole?*

What choice did I have? I couldn't have them arrested. Also, when I moved out, they weren't elderly. Then they were.

My mother liked the story of the Collyer brothers, eccentric New York millionaires who collected books and paper and detritus. The way she told the story, one was killed when a pile of books fell over and crushed him; his brother, an invalid, then starved to death. She invoked the Collyer brothers when she thought my father should get rid of some books or maybe find shelves for them.

Fire, book collapse, flood. At any moment a disaster could befall my parents. Or, worse, nothing definitive would happen, and I would have to make an assessment and a decision: *No, you cannot live here another day. I don't know where you'll go, but this place will kill you, the house has given you that cough, the house is the reason the wound on your leg won't heal—wait, you have a wound on your leg that won't heal, too? The house doesn't love you; the house wants you dead. I love you and want you alive.* Easier to blame the house than my parents, who had let it lapse into this state. Monstrous house: It had eaten my parents and was digesting them.

When I was a grown-up but still young, I imagined that my parents would eventually face facts and move to a nice apartment in the Back Bay, near their jobs at BU. Maybe they'd give up their car and take cabs. A doorman building, with an elevator. Fresh walls for the art. A spare room with a sofa bed and shelves for books. They already had a sofa bed, purchased from Castro Convertibles, upholstered in a fabric called Herculon. They had the books and the art. All they needed was to get rid of a few things. I thought they might do it.

Weekends they drove to Maine and Western Massachusetts and bought antiques: entire encyclopedias, oak rocking chairs. Their own parents died, and household goods moved in like a series of avalanches. Stuff got crammed in till leaving seemed impossible. Some cousins only a little older sold their house and moved into an assisted-living complex. My mother was embarrassed for them.

For a long time my parents got rid of nothing. The rooms filled with objects and garbage, luggage and inherited love letters, cats. In my childhood there had been a lot of animals—four cats and two dogs at the height—but in my parents' older age it was only ever cats and only ever two. My mother's favorite cats were male and nervous and needed her. "Come to Mommy," my mother would say to one of them. "Yes, I love you, too."

"You are not that cat's mother," I said, sitting on the sofa during a visit.

"Don't listen to her," said my mother.

I won't point out the obvious—that my mother never said she loved me—because it's academic. My mother loved me. It's not a question. I knew it and she knew it. Her inability to say so felt no different from her inability, her refusal, to speak French. Once in a restaurant in Paris, she stubbornly ordered "the chicken soup," even though *bouillon* was a word I'd heard her say dozens of times, followed by the word *cube*. The closest to a foreign language I ever heard her speak, apart from a smattering of Yiddish, was also really English: When a waiter delivered her plate in Paris, she said *messy* to him. In Rome, *grassy.* Saying the words was the problem. Love, too: She knew what it meant, even if she couldn't pronounce it.

Still, I wish she had stumbled a little in saying it to the cat.

My parents were a sight gag. Opposites otherwise, too. One shy but given to monologues, one outgoing and inclined to listen. One with a temper; one affable, sometimes enragingly so. Opposite in every way but their bad habits, which is the secret to a happy marriage and also the makings of a catastrophe.

Early Sunday morning, and the street outside Trevor's was silent, as he said it would be: We were near the City of London, the old square-mile city, which cleared out on weekends, when the businessfolk went home. The air smelled as though a river of beer ran close by, though the weather had broken enough that heat wouldn't be the story of the day. On the next-door stoop, someone had left a crate of empty milk bottles, glass, with bent-back foil caps. I was sorry the milkman—the milkman! A character from a children's book, the milkman, the sandman, the muffin man—hadn't been by so I could steal a bottle and drink the milk down, feel the cold of the glass on my lip and the different, thicker cold of the milk on the inside of my cheeks. There are certain emotions available to me only when I am alone, minor longings and notions, a wish to filch and misbehave. This is either my truest self or my most artificial, constructed as it is without a fear of contradiction. Even a single person on the street would have interfered with these thoughts. Above the empty bottles, a note flapped out of the mail slot, the words written in failing felt-tip pen, split on the curves: *No milk today, please.*

Around the corner, the hanging green that Trevor had promised was not green at all but paved over, empty of people. That morning he'd given me a long history of Clerkenwell, punctuated by restaurant recommendations; I hadn't paid attention. Lenin and Stalin had met in a nearby pub, except that I'd initially heard *Lennon* and waited for *McCartney* or *Brian Epstein*, and by the time I'd located my brain's wrong turn, I was lost. There was a Belgian bar nearby and also quite a good Italian, and nuns used to walk in underground tunnels to church. Cromwell, according to Trevor, had done . . . something in the neighborhood. Smashed a stained-glass window. Lived, perhaps.

I had my pocketbook slung over my shoulder. If something were to happen to me, if I pitched off a bridge into the river, my pocketbook swept away, who would they contact, and how would they find that person? *L'inconnue du Thames,* they'd call me. *I saw you walking,* people told me at home, stunned. In my Texas neighborhood there weren't even sidewalks; I missed them. As a child in Massachusetts, I'd had a profound relationship with the pavement. In my memory I never looked ahead but at my feet, at the handprints and paw prints and scrawled initials, the lines and cracks that I dodged in honor of my mother's already unusual spine and back, at the tree-root-humped blocks that tilted like wings of a drawbridge. The sidewalk of my suburban youth was like God, omnipresent and irregular. In Texas, where I'd lived for a decade, walking was seen as a form of peculiarity, perhaps a sign of northern-ness, even among my largely unarmed Texan friends. Sometimes in Texas as I walked, I would suddenly feel the presence of all the hidden guns around me, as though I were an x-ray machine. Here in London, I knew that not a single civilian—or police officer, for that matter—was armed.

Already I was lost. But there was a sign at the edge of the ungreen green that showed the neighborhood: what was within a five-minute walk of *You are here,* what within a fifteen-minute. Some things only the city itself can tell you, and other things you must learn from a map. In Austin there are enormous streets called Lanes, as well as Drives and Streets and Circles and Boulevards; in my mother's suburban Boston neighborhood, dead ends called Terraces. Trevor's place was on a Close, and I was headed for Jerusalem Passage. Surely I would be changed upon it. I passed the Belgian bar Trevor had mentioned, now closed. A shared workspace, closed. Early Sunday morning in the business district: Everything was closed.

That was good. I was walking. I was a walker. In some cities you can still see the old districts, meat and music, diamonds, garments, though now every city is mostly the automatic-teller district, the mobile-phone district. Where was I? I tried to intuit which way the Thames was. Then I could navigate.

An enormous stone many-windowed building with a central arch presented itself. A train station, except not. Above the arch, two silver dragons glowered down. The visiting American (*this* visiting American) will note that London is full of incidental mythical animals, wyverns and hippogriffs and common-as-dirt unicorns. I walked through the arch; the dragons watched me go. This was Smithfield, the meat market, though the butchers were at home or in church, gates pulled over the stalls like eyelids. Only the smell of animal blood remained. It made me hungry, a little sick. I hurried to get out.

Around the corner, a municipal worker paused his sidewalk power-washing so I could pass. He didn't smile. A lady cyclist, pleated skirt (black), tucked in T-shirt (palest pink), no helmet, no makeup, a beauty, came whistling by, resonant and cheery. Her shoes were spacesuit silver and caught the light as she pedaled. Whistling like a man. Now, why did I think that? Did fewer women whistle loudly because of an anatomical difference or societal pressure? Perhaps I, a congenital and disappointed non-whistler, could with my eventual inheritance from the sale of my mother's house fund a school for girls, a conservatory of feminine, feminist whistlers, and name it for my mother. My mother had achieved a lot in her life, mostly by ignoring the muttering people who suggested that she might be incapable of things because of her body or gender or religion. She was proudly aware of the things she couldn't do: spell, navigate. She couldn't whistle, or, for that matter, snap. I could snap.

A muddling sound down the street, as though something small were being pulverized by an enormous pestle. I couldn't make it out till I got closer and the sound grew louder: The bells of St. Paul's were bashing the morning to bits. I came around the corner and there was the cathedral, as startling as an elk in the road. I hadn't realized I was that near. I tried to find the pattern in the bells, but it was only ringing, only loveliness, only metal sounding in stone. Moments before, as I passed the power-washing man and the whistling woman passed me, I hadn't known exactly where I was. Now I was a pin on the map.

This was where my mother and I had stayed, three years before, in an unglamorous but accessible hotel just to my left. I had over-researched it, as I over-researched everything concerning travel. As a traveler, I was not carefree.

My mother and I had different philosophies of hotel life. I'd examined pictures on the internet of the green chair in Trevor's Room No. 2 a dozen times before booking; I'd read reviews that called it *adorable* and *dark;* I'd performed numerous calculations on the abacus of my soul concerning the price of the room and the loveliness of the slipper tub. My mother, on the other hand, declared that a hotel room was a place to sleep and nothing else. She was terrible with money and pinched pennies to convince herself that she wasn't. My mother hated being bad at anything that involved reason. Once, I had to rescue her and my father from a highway-side motel in Austin where every other guest had come because it was a convenient place to procure drugs. My mother had not wanted to be rescued; rescue would suggest she hadn't made a good decision, and anyhow, she didn't mind dives. My father, like me, favored grand hotels and the bars therein.

This hotel, the one I'd stayed in with my mother, wasn't grand, but it was much nicer than a dive, accessible for the motorized scooter my mother then used to get around. The room was long and doglegged, a sort of one-room suite, with a bed by the door and a pullout couch by the window and a bathroom between the two. My mother took the couch; the actual bed was too high for her to get into. She'd turn eighty-two in two months, was full of energy for all things but also was small and stiff. My father was three years dead. I knew how to help my mother when we traveled together, what assistance she needed and what she didn't and what was intrusive. Years before this I had invented a method I called the Footjack, in which, when she was going up stairs, I would stand behind her and stick my foot under her foot and bring it up to the target stair, and while you can never know what it feels like to be in somebody else's body, in this case I had an intimation of one aspect: I could feel all through my leg how stiff her leg was that day. Sometimes it was a cinch to raise her foot. Other times I had to use all my muscle, while my mother winced, said, "No, keep going." Every time I performed the Footjack, she said, "Your father claims he invented this, but it was you." One of the minor sorrows of her old age was her inability to stay in a hotel room by herself; the biggest problem was that she couldn't get onto her scooter unaided. I was about to say, *But she didn't dwell on it,* but who knows what another person dwells upon? In our London hotel room, I dreamt all night of the subway trains barreling beneath us, until I realized we were on the fourth floor and my bed shared a wall with the elevator shaft.

On that trip I climbed to the top of St. Paul's by myself while my mother got dressed and brushed her teeth in the room, a little time all alone. I went up the stairs to the hem of the dome. Looking down into the cathedral from the Whispering Gallery unnerved me. There shouldn't be such heights inside buildings. I kept going to the higher exterior galleries—Stone, Golden. I've always liked to climb things on my own, a kind of vacation from life on earth, a way to meditate (I guess; I don't meditate) on breath and elevation and doggedness. My mother never needed to meditate on doggedness: She was dogged. "I am dogged, you are stubborn, she is pigheaded," my mother might say, one of her favorite word games. I preferred to climb towers and obelisks, to be locked in stone until the top, when I'd be rewarded with wind and view. There was such a tower nearby, a memorial to the victims of the Great Fire of London, but my mother was waiting for me. She couldn't climb stairs at all by then, never mind the 528 of St. Paul's.

This morning, this very morning, August 2019, a Sunday, I had grown stouter and gammy of knee, and I wouldn't climb, and my mother was dead, and I walked past St. Paul's Cathedral. Sunday, the cathedral ringing itself like a bell. Sunday, so I would not go in. I wasn't a churchgoer, nor was my little Yiddishe mama, who'd been brought up with Hebrew school and weekly services and passed none of it on to me. The story of my youth was different: I went to matinees at the Paramount Theater down the street. My mother and I liked churches for their touristic possibilities, filled as they were with sculpture, stained glass, cool in the summertime, dark, occasional music, candlelight, needlepoint. We didn't like church when it was in session. (Church was always in session for churchgoers.) My father had been a churchgoer as a child but never afterward. He didn't believe in God. He believed less the older he got. How could you, he thought, when suffering was all around.

When I was thirty-five years old—a long time ago, when the millennium was new—I decided to clean my parents' kitchen. This was the old kitchen, the one I'd grown up with, purple walls and intermittent lurid wallpaper (tropical, orange and yellow, a little purple to pick up the color of the paint). Comically outdated even in 1974, when we moved in; we made jokes about it. I no longer remember what the counters were like. They might have been white and speckled with gold, or white and squared off with brown seams at the edges, or patterned like an old man's pajamas.

The floor, though, is clear in my memory, a faux Roman mosaic made up of larger tiles. I liked to stare at it to appreciate the individual bits, how the smaller pattern built the larger pattern, the way tiles had been turned to join up with others. I still have this habit with all floors. I would theorize that this means something about my brain or philosophy or life's work—*look for small motifs that build into something larger*—but it's only ever been floors.

My childhood kitchen tile: the lost linoleum of Pompeii. I would clean it last. The room was crowded with furniture: a yellow enamel-top cabinet next to the fridge, an oak table inherited from a friend in the center, and what my mother called a Hoosier cabinet against the far wall, the sort of thing that might have been new in the kitchen of her youth. (At antique stores, my father bought Victoriana. My mother liked things from her own childhood: the breadboard with a picture of Uncle Sam captioned *It's Patriotic to Slice Your Own;* a statue of FDR as boat captain, hands on a ship's wheel that was also a clock.) (To be fair, my father's childhood was probably fairly Victorian in feel.)

It's difficult to organize even thoughts, standing as I am mentally in my parents' kitchen. The Hoosier cabinet was tall, everything an early-to-mid-twentieth-century American housewife was supposed to need: drawers for cutlery, a rolltop front that hid pigeonholes, a door that looked ordinary but tilted out to reveal a flour sifter. The past was full of sifted flour. My parents stored things on top of the cabinet, the brown and gold Le Creuset pans they'd bought at Bloomingdale's in the late 1970s, the Georges Briard enamelware they'd received as a wedding present in 1959, everything now wearing little cloaks of dust. More than dust—the dense gray matter that accumulates in an old house with cats in it, opaque and oddly damp.

I began. Off went the cloaks of dust. On went Murphy Oil Soap: cabinet doors, the clattering rolltop, the sides. I moved from counter to counter, appliance to cupboard. (Cup board: This is where the cups board.) I scrubbed the slanted hood over the stove, which perhaps had never really been cleaned in the years of my parents' residence. My mother couldn't clean it. My father wouldn't.

"Don't throw anything out," my mother had told me. She was home as I labored, sitting on her favored corner of the sofa, feet propped up on the coffee table (she was so short her legs didn't reach the floor). She would have been sixty-seven then. How is this possible? I know how time and math work, but I'd forgotten my mother was ever so young—and by young I don't mean thirty-two; I mean sixty-seven. Her hair was still long. (I'll tell you about my mother's hair; she'd like that.) That she was home meant it was the weekend. She worked long hours during the week. She wouldn't have let me clean when she wasn't there. I wasn't to be trusted.

I brought her, cradled in my arms, the three waffle irons I'd uncovered on the kitchen counter.

"Three," I told her, as though they were a litter.

"Yes," said my mother.

"Which one do you want to keep?"

"All of them."

I don't think my mother formally collected waffle irons (though later I would find an antique one beneath her bed), and at the moment I wanted—I so often wanted—her to face the contradictory facts of her existence, which in this case were that she and my father, then still alive, had accumulated too many objects and never ate breakfast at home and yet owned three waffle irons. My mother's dislike of breakfast was something she herself held dear; she liked to tell the story of how she had for the first week of her marriage made breakfast every day, until my father admitted that the thought of food first thing in the morning made him a little sick, too. A legendary story. My mother was very good at turning anecdotes into legend. She loved to tell stories about herself.

"You don't need three waffle irons," I told her, rattling the collection in my arms.

She looked at me. No, she didn't: *She looked at me* is one of those phrases that falls into prose, into fiction—this isn't a memoir—around dialogue. *She looked away, she sighed, she raised her eyebrows, tears filled her eyes.* My mother felt that the number of waffle irons she owned was a personal issue. Her private business. Why was I poking my nose in? She distrusted anything that invaded privacy. Mental-health professionals of any kind, for instance. If you were really in trouble, if you'd broken down entirely, then it might be OK, but psychotherapy was like trying to fix a motor while it was still running.

What good was understanding your own mind if you jammed it in the process? She was volubly contemptuous about therapy, and about memoirs that complained about parents, about complaining about parents in general. She liked to quote her favorite *New Yorker* cartoon, a man on an analyst's couch, saying, "I had a difficult childhood, especially lately." My mother was known to say with disgust, "Oh, those people who write memoirs about the worst thing that ever happened to them!" I said it, too. Some years later a terrible thing happened to me, and there was nothing to do but to write a memoir. It was an accident, I swear on my mother's grave, which doesn't exist, and won't, though she is dead: She didn't believe in graves, or memoirs about parents, was suspicious of a writer who might start such a book before (as my mother would say) the corpse was cold. It's worse than that, I might tell my mother now: Such books start before there is a corpse. They start in the hospital, or on the plane to the city where the hospital is located. They start the minute life looks fragile. It might sound stonehearted, but it's only a way to keep the person close. Not as close as in life, impossible, but also in some ways closer. I'm not saying it's selfless. It's greedy. It's one of the greediest things I know.

No, my mother didn't look at me. She never just sat on the sofa: There was always something that needed her attention. She ran the publications department at Boston University; chances are she was marking up an article for the alumni magazine that she edited or hemming a pair of pants. She would have looked at whatever she was doing, would have said, of the waffle makers, "They're all different."

Technically that was true: one that worked on a stove top; an old-fashioned plug-in model with a fabric-wrapped cord; a deep-pocketed Belgian number; all intended to mint waffles and nothing else. I said, with a note of hysteria, "When was the last time you even *made* waffles?"

"I make waffles all the time. Put them back," she said, and I did, though away in a cabinet.

I cleared off counters. I consolidated the mind-boggling amounts of spare change that followed my parents wherever they went, a minor myth, a tinkling train of not-much money. Everything they touched turned to nickels. I sponged off knickknacks, including the owls that my mother collected, still a manageable quantity. Soon enough they would become an infestation caused by the good intentions and generosity of the many people who adored her. In her last years she said to me, "No more owls." There was no stopping the owls, owl after owl after owl. She liked to sing, *"Owl be seeing you in all the old familiar places."*

I threw out corroded batteries, used and unused. I tossed plastic containers that had lost their lids and lids that had lost their plastic containers. I turned to the fridge. Once we had a glorious cat who could open a fridge door with a claw; one year he let himself in and shut the door behind him and ate half a cooked turkey breast and meowed to get out. The length of elastic my father had attached to thereafter tie the fridge shut still dangled from the handle, though the cat himself was long gone. I binned what was past its expiration date or blackened or greened or liquefied by time, the ancient takeout cartons, the former strawberries. All the humors of the condiments clung to the mouths of their bottles and jars: gummy dark ketchup, gluey mustard, phlegmatic mayonnaise. At the back of the fridge I found an unopened brick of cheese, three years out of date.

Back to the living room. I brandished the cheese. "Three years out of date!" I said to my mother.

Her expression was momentarily shocked. Then she found an answer. "No," she explained. "I just bought that."

"1999!" I said. "Look!"

"Printer's error," said my mother, who generally used her considerable powers of stubbornness for good.

"I'm throwing it out."

"I just—"

"I'm throwing it out," I told her.

I don't mean to suggest that my parents never cleaned anything. My *father* never cleaned anything, I don't think. But my mother did, even though it was difficult for her. By then they could have afforded to hire somebody, but it seemed too late, the disorder too embarrassing to be seen even by a professional. They were still sleeping upstairs, or mostly were, but the buildup of objects meant that they stuck to a few rooms: the living room, the kitchen, their bedroom, the downstairs bath. All other rooms were waist-high or higher with things. Meteorological, a blizzard of objects now frozen into tunnels.

(Four years after I cleaned the kitchen, a semi-miracle occurred. My parents hired a bunch of people to clear out the downstairs rooms so that they could be remodeled, even the kitchen. My father referred to the cleaning crew as the Barbarians. Like any strangers who came into the house, they irked my father with their very presence. When we moved in, he'd built floor-to-ceiling bookshelves throughout the house, including the dining room, back when it was the dining room, uncharacteristic behavior for him in both physical enterprise and handiness, but my parents owned thousands of books, which needed to go somewhere. When the garbage and the Barbarians receded from the dining room, the bookshelves were off-kilter, rhomboid. "I built those shelves on Gothic principles," my father said. Meaning: Notre Dame still stood; surely my father's shelves would have persisted, too, without the intervention of the irksome Barbarians.)

A pattern. In my parents and on the kitchen tile. Yes, my mother cleaned sometimes. She mopped the floor. She had a weakness for Future floor polish, which made the tile so shiny it looked wet; walking across a just-mopped floor was one of the only things I did that made her really mad. ("At least do it in stocking feet.") Futured, the tile gleamed like the floors of a proposed space station in a mid-century book about late-century life. Futuristic. Then the floors dulled and yellowed, like any vision of what's to come.

As I scrubbed the fake mosaic, I could see the arc of my mother's mopping. I fought past the layers of all the substances she used to clean—the Future, the Pine-Sol, the sandy residue of Spic and Span. My mother was short and moved with difficulty, and my father should have mopped the floors, or they should have engaged some-body. No wonder she never got under the furniture or to the baseboards, where the floor was dark, the detail of the tile gone.

I scrubbed. I applied hot water. I scrabbled, using my nails as implements. (I have never found any clean-ing tool as effective as fingernails.) My hands ached. All parts of me ached—I would spend the next day in bed as a result of this labor, which was a declaration of love for my parents and also for a man I'd just met and al-ready knew was essential; I was trying to make a house he could visit without being appalled, a house my parents could welcome a stranger into without it being the end of the world. I had never brought anyone home to my parents. He would be the first and only.

The blackness on the floor gave way. I wore it down. I hit something. Beneath the layers of filth, no other word for it, I could see small curves, then circles, then coins.

Quarters. Fallen to the ground how long ago? Then covered by the weather of the house, by which I mean dirt so thick nobody knew they were there at all.

If you want to write a memoir without writing a memoir, go ahead and call it something else. Let other people argue about it. Arguing with yourself or the dead will get you nowhere.

Imagine a character who can't profess her love; how do things change if you show the one moment she can?

When I turned toward the river from the side of St. Paul's, London seemed heaving with humanity at last, the Millennium Bridge a shifting snake with every tourist a scale. I would cross the bridge—Tate Modern was just the other side—but first I took a set of stairs down to the Thames promenade to get a closer look at the river, which even so was kept behind a wall. From the promenade, you could get down to the actual foreshore via some steps—not quite a staircase, not quite a ladder, some mixture of the two, a stairder, a ladcase. I couldn't picture myself upon it. Instead, I looked at the mudlarks on the foreshore and listened to an elderly woman behind me lecture another elderly person on the subject of birds. "All herons are egrets," she said, "but not all egrets herons."

The mudlarks themselves were people. A noun, a verb: Mudlarks mudlark. That is, they look for the objects the river has held on to for decades or centuries and has, at low tide, decided to disclose. Coins, but they know it. Bits of pottery. The people of the past were always chucking things in bodies of water, messages in bottles, except the bottle was the message: a bit of brown glass that says *wine*, a bit of green glass that says *gin*. Any number of clay pipes incised with the maker's initials. Teeth. Jawbones of sheep. That morning the mudlarks were men and eleven-year-old boys, those ubiquitous hobbyists (hobby shops are aimed at traditionally masculine pastimes, craft shops at feminine), but also middle-aged women and young ones. They walked with hunched purpose. They kicked at the shore, then stopped. They hoped for a Tudor shoe or a Roman ring, the mud churned up to reveal a winking edge.

To stop walking felt awful. I turned from the river and saw something I hadn't noticed on my way down, a glass box, an elevator that ran at a slant alongside the stairs. Life with my mother had trained me to see the world in terms of accessibility and inaccessibility. Sometimes you were surprised by an ingenious solution. My mother would have loved this elevator. I looked left and right and thought self-righteously about my complaining knee, and I pressed the button and the glass doors parted and I boarded.

THE MILLENNIUM INCLINATOR, a plaque on the wall said. Funny name for a funicular.

It began its ascent. I was going to say *inexorable ascent*, but of course it would stop when it got to the top. It was just very slow. I was a middle-aged woman with uncombed hair in a glass box; I decided to pretend that it and I were a performance piece. Up at the top—at my destination—a mother and small child stood by their stroller. I drew closer in my box. At first I thought they were pointing at me; then I realized they were pointing only at the Inclinator. I was invisible inside it, unnoteworthy. The child was wearing a blowsy rose-patterned dress that suited her and would have also suited her great-grandmother. She had the kind of exceptionally blond hair, flaxen, that mostly didn't exist in America but was as common as flax here. Her mother was dressed in various gauzy gray layers that hid where one garment began and another took over and where she herself ended and began, a Möbius mother, very chic and unknowable. All mothers are unknowable, being a subset of human beings. Mother and daughter peered into my box with concentration. I waved. The girl waved back. By the time I arrived, she was thrilled to see me.

"WHAT'S YOUR NAME," she bellowed, in the curiously deep voice some English children have.

"I don't have one," I told her. "I am nameless."

"No you're not," she said.

"No, I'm not," I admitted. Like any nameless narrator,

I've just declined to introduce myself. I apologize if you hate such narrators and such novels. We have this in common. *I* hate novels with unnamed narrators. I didn't mean to write one. Write enough books and these things will happen. I never meant to write a novel about a writer, either. I vowed not to. Writers are dull by themselves, intolerable when they gather. Intolerable always. I find myself intolerable, the author of these sentences, which means I am writing a book about a writer.

"Everybody has a name," the child told me. "Even my brother."

The stroller wasn't hers; it was full of baby. I put my hand across the elevator doorjamb so that the doors wouldn't bite them as they went through, a habit from traveling with my mother.

"My brother just vomited all over the Tube," the girl said.

"Brothers'll do that," I answered. The baby in his stroller was a very Caesar. "Widi Wici Womit."

The mother was older than I'd expected, not as old as me, but close. Her hair was in a topknot. I try not to be judgmental about how other people comb their hair, but I can't abide a topknot. She gave me an appraising look that let me know she was actually the grandmother and said, disapprovingly, "Quite a character."

"Not really," I agreed. Then I realized she meant the little girl.

They boarded the Inclinator. I watched their stately

declination away from me. If they'd turned to look, I would have waved.

Of course I have a name. My mother gave it to me, the name of a beloved cousin, alive at the time of my birth. When I mentioned this fact, which I had always known, to my mother's mother, she was aghast. "Your mother would never do that!" my grandmother said. "Jews don't do that! You were named after your father's sister." My father's sister was also alive, but Gentile, so that was allowed.

The curve of the Millennium Bridge had made it look more packed than it was, though there were plenty of people upon it and 47 percent of them were taking photographs.

Myself, I loathe having my picture taken. I have for as long as I can remember, even in the old days when you could go weeks without somebody trying. In all group shots I am *not pictured*. It's beyond vanity and in the realm of superstition. I don't like people looking at me. I don't like being the center of attention except under very specific conditions. Then I adore it. That's why I prefer fiction to memoir. I am unable to render my own character in words, having no idea of what my character is, beyond certain bad habits. My understanding of my own soul is preliterate. *Wife, daughter, mother, friend,* some people write in their social-media biographies. Why on earth? Applying any words to who I am feels like a straight pin aimed at my insect self. I won't have it. I can't do it.

I will not stop for a photo. I will not look at myself in a mirror for you. I will not watch myself pass in a plate-glass window or imagine what a stranger thinks upon seeing me.

On the Millennium Bridge the tourists of the world documented themselves. A doll family with black hair and dark eyes, all the same height, a teenage boy operating the selfie stick, the father in a pompadour—it cheered me that a pompadour could exist in a twenty-first-century marriage. A red-mustachioed man in a Coca-Cola T-shirt, kneeling to photograph his glamorous mother, whose miniskirt showed just the dimpling dumpling undercurve of her thighs. She wore a blue knee brace that matched her high heels. Teenage girls together. A pair of sixty-ish women, one plump, one narrow, their arms around each other, the thin woman holding a phone out. For many years I had a place among these people: I was asked to take photographs, a single woman who looked competent, honest, and not fleet of foot enough to take off with a camera. But the world no longer needed me this way.

I slowed but I didn't stop. I strode out. "Well, that's ruined it," I heard a woman mutter as I passed.

She was examining the screen of her camera—an actual camera, not a phone; she took herself seriously—and she wanted me to feel bad. The wind was pulling apart her ponytail in a quarrelsome way. I didn't feel bad; I felt marvelous. For years I'd been polite around tourists taking pictures. I'd yielded, believing as many people did then, and some still do, that this was the moral law. It was one of the wonders of the modern age, the ability to not give a fuck about ruining other people's photographs, the selfies, the selfie sticks, the beloveds on bridges or in front of famous paintings. That day, I broke all the little chains linking photographer and subject. I am terribly rude. *Excuse me,* I said (my terrible rudeness wears a disguise of politeness) as I walked into frame. I felt the enlivening tension, the giving way. It was a pleasure to ruin other people's photographs. It felt like clearing out the underbrush, picking up litter on the point of a stick. One less, one less.

Below me the tide was coming in, threatening the mudlarks. If I threw myself in (I wasn't going to throw myself in), would the currents take me away and bring me back to the mudlarkers in a year, or forty, or a century? Would my shoes—sandals from the "comfort" shoe store, meaning *comfortable,* not *comforting*—be displayed in a museum of artifacts? If the world hadn't already ended, I amended, as I amended all future times in my head.

By *the world* I meant human beings, as human beings do. The Thames would still be here with nobody to comb it for treasures. It would seethe on, full of teeth.

My mother told stories about her hair. It was pitch black—though blacker than pitch itself, which is merely dark brown. The black of outer space or of ravens, the black of black-and-white photographs. It was so black that when in the late 1950s a New York friend painted his bathroom black, my mother could not see her hair in the mirror to comb it. Left to its natural state, it was what in hair circles used to be called *unmanageable*. I've just washed my hair and I can't do a thing with it. Who wants to manage hair? Even in childhood pictures, when my meticulous grandmother had ironed and perfected everything else, overalls and hair bows, tiny ankle socks, my mother's hair asserts itself, a confusion of curls.

She was in New York because she was a theater person:

She wanted to direct. The year she lived in the city, she was getting an MA from Columbia. Her letters home to that little whistle-stop Iowa town discuss her wardrobe in depth. Her parents' clothing store, originally full of overalls for railroad men, was now a women's apparel shop. My mother asked for pieces of her extensive wardrobe to be shipped to her—tights, a belt, a peach dress—and said she'd be happy for new clothes, too. One of the recurring characters in the letters was an aging gray skirt she despised and depended upon. She was directing plays then, too, though there is no detail about them: *enclosed find an ad for the play, the play will run another weekend, the play will run three weeks or one night, depending.*

I'm getting deep into the Scandinavians, she said in one letter, and signed another, *Love, Mrs. Strindberg.*

In one of her last emails to me, she told me her days had been dull but busy. *"The dirt of life," Strindberg called all the little tasks that consume time better given in his case to writing plays. But then he thought his cook was stealing nutrition from his food.*

I was talking about her hair. Another story: In high school, after she'd had a bad haircut, the yearbook photographer gave up. No matter what, my mother's hair would not behave, as hair and teenage girls were supposed to. "I'll fix it later," he told my mother, and airbrushed in somebody else's hairdo, shellacked and orderly. That might have been the last time she got her hair cut for decades.

It must have driven her tidy mother crazy. My mother's mother, a native brunette, had her hair washed and set every week. By the time I knew her, she was a champagne blonde. My mother went in the opposite direction, which was, as with many opposite directions, not altogether unlike. She didn't put a toe past the threshold of a beauty parlor (as they were called back then; *pizza, ice cream, funeral, tattoo, beauty,* what do these things have in common besides *parlor*?). Not ever, never mind once a week. But her hair had to be attended to in very particular ways. She washed it in the kitchen sink, with thick emerald Prell. I can still smell Prell, I can nearly taste it, the crenelated white cap, the slowness of its movements. Do women still wash their hair in the kitchen sink? She had a little step stool (she could get up on a step stool when I was a kid) so she could lean over and use the sprayer to chase the lather from her hair. Then she sat in her corner of the sofa with it loose around her shoulders while it air-dried, which took hours. She said, "I look like Tiny Tim." The Tiny Tim with a ukulele, not the one with a crutch. (She loved the singer Tiny Tim, whom she recognized as one of her people: joyful and oddball.) Every morning she combed her hair into an elaborate bun. Divide the hair into sections. Pull the front part back first. Then start coiling. Fasten each coil with an extra-long hairpin, the kind that must be mail-ordered (before everything in the world was mail-ordered) or found in the back of an old-fashioned drugstore. A skein of hair from one side of the head, then the other. Don't rush it. You can do anything, my mother liked to say, once you've figured out a system. Where had she learned how to do it? From a theater friend, probably. She wove her hair into a basket, as elaborate as the blond confection my grandmother's hairdresser spun her hair into once a week in far-off Des Moines.

It must have been quite good for my mother's flexibility, to stretch her arms that way every morning.

My grandmother was a nonpracticing lawyer, not the first woman to graduate from Benjamin Harrison Law School in Indianapolis but the only one in the class of 1927. She was president of her sisterhood, traveled as a public speaker, needlepointed, knit, took photographs and developed them, was a small-business consultant, silk-screened tablecloths, once built a table, and still had time to worry too much. Somewhere there's a picture of me in a sweater set of such burlappy awfulness, steel wool to the eye as well as the skin, so cunningly unflattering to every proportion of the short, plump 1980s teenager I was, you would have thought it had been designed as a specific punishment, not knit out of love, though she did love me, which is why the photo exists: She wanted me to pose engulfed in proof.

Still, I knew that my mother was her darling. They had been through a lot together. When we visited, my grandmother would rush to unbutton my mother's coat for her and bought her treats, like raspberries in season, that nobody else was allowed to eat. Every year my Jewish grandmother sent us Easter baskets, the largest for my mother: I remember staring, furious and uncomprehending, at the size of her chocolate rabbit.

Though my mother was a feminist—indeed, she thought that women were smarter and tougher than men in every way—she had a few failings of her time. My father preferred long hair on women; my mother wore her hair long and kept my hair long until I finally badgered her into letting me have a fourth-grade Dorothy Hamill. Thereafter she trimmed my bangs, the usual parental atrocity, at a slant this way, a slant that way, even them up . . . damnation. "Damnation what?" I would ask. Knowing what I do now about my mother's coordination and eye for detail, I can't imagine why she tried, apart from her flabbergasting self-confidence and frugality.

Only once did she let me cut her hair. I was in high school and had recently read an old guide to all-natural hair care, illustrated with R. Crumb–style drawings. How to be a hippie, but not a dirty one. (As a teenager I loved the 1960s, which seemed like the distant past, though I was *born* during the sixties, for heaven's sake.) Among the things the hair-care book had taught me: Use rosemary oil on your boar-bristle brush for shiny, fragrant locks; if you never trim your hair, it will stop growing.

"It'll *look* like it's stopped growing," my mother said.

"What do you mean?"

"Hair grows from your head. The roots don't know what's going on at the ends. The book means that if you don't cut your hair, it'll break off at the ends, and it'll *seem* like it's stopped growing. OK, ducks," she said. "Give my hair a trim."

My hands in the otherworld of my mother's hair. She sat at the kitchen table and I stood behind her. Silver then, and not exactly wavy, not exactly curly, though as I pulled it straight so I could even it up (I wouldn't exact my revenge), it went from below her shoulder blades to below her waist. Is there any feminine mystery greater than the differences between a mother's body and a daughter's? The flat-chested generation giving life to the bosomy, the delicate-footed to the size thirteen? Why does God let it happen? What does it mean?

As I walked along the Thames, the London Eye came into view—impossible though it seems that it could ever be out of view or that I had forgotten it existed. The London Eye is a vast Ferris wheel that completes one revolution in half an hour, a clock that turns its passengers into time. All things are new that were built when I was grown up, though I've been a grown-up for more than three-fifths of my life: I'm incapable of recognizing the Boston skyline. My mother liked the amusement-park rides she'd had to leave behind in her youth; she lamented the inflexibility that prevented her from folding into a bumper car, with its ideal single pedal, its pleasurable spinning. (Once, at Paragon Park on Nantasket Beach in Massachusetts, my father offered to take me on the bumper cars, but when we arrived at the rink I turned out to be too short, and then my father did something inconceivable to me: He went on by himself and made me watch him bump other people's children, and at the end he got himself so trapped in the small around-the-chest safety strap, the teenager who ran the ride had to wrench him out.)

I hadn't climbed St. Paul's, but I could still look down on the city, as one among many in a glass bubble. "Over there," said the red-vested woman in front of the Eye, pointing to an ancient impressive stone building opposite. There I purchased a ticket from a machine, a *kiosk*, a word I had once loved but now was everywhere and just meant *stationary robot*. Fast track for an extra fee? Absolutely. I was a person who would spend anything to avoid standing in line; I was a sucker made for the modern age. I ran my card and waited, as I always did, for the computer to refuse, to reveal I had accidentally spent everything, emptied every bank account, spent all my credit and was ruined. Then I heard the nibbling zip of the machine printing out my ticket, and all was well.

The London Eye turned so slowly that you had to concentrate to see it move, clockwise or counterclockwise depending on which bank of the Thames you stood on. I got in the fast-track line—*make way, I'm important*— and eyeballed the school trips in the other, longer line. A bother of pubescent children in matching red T-shirts; a gang of teenagers with matching green knapsacks. They didn't notice me in my black knit dress, my gray knit leggings, my comfort sandals. Like many people, I felt most conspicuous when most invisible: the terror of suddenly springing into view. My mother didn't care, because she had no choice. She was conspicuous. Perhaps this is what made her a theater person: might as well be purposeful. She acted in her youth, though only in parts that didn't require her to walk onstage. She would find her mark in the dark, the curtains would open, she would deliver a monologue, the curtains would close. As a kid, I could imagine it, thrilling, even though I never saw her act. I had once wanted to be a theater person but failed. I auditioned and was not cast, not in *The Mousetrap*, or *God*, or *A Lesson from Aloes*, or any of the many high school plays I tried out for. Chances are I was terrible, both a show-off and paralytically shy, my clothing peculiar, a kid incapable of being anyone but herself. One day, I rushed to the door of the school theater and at last saw my name on the cast list: I had been given a nonspeaking role as an oyster in *Alice in Wonderland*. I declined the part and never auditioned again.

On days like this, I felt I might be an actress, playing the part of a stranger in other people's lives. We tourists were portioned into smaller lines, then ushered into cars. Capsules, the London Eye called them, suggesting space travel and 1970s cold medicine. The capsules didn't pause at the platform. You had to step in as your designated car rotated minutely or semi-minutely away from you. I felt the fluttering hand of a young man at my elbow; I was old enough that I might need assistance. Then I was aboard, and the doors closed behind me and my capsule-mates. Capsule number 14, which was really capsule number 13, like the thirteenth floor in some hotels, as though bad luck can't count. Twice recently I'd stayed on the so-called fourteenth and therefore thirteenth floor in a hotel, and I'd wanted to complain, not because I was superstitious but because I wasn't a rube, except I was superstitious and I was a rube, so I didn't complain, and I couldn't complain now, either, because we were revolving away from the young people who ran the thing. There must have been a single person in a booth somewhere, as for any carnival ride, who could pull a lever or depress a pedal or push a button to stop the thing.

After I failed at acting, I concentrated on writing. In college I had one particularly influential teacher, in whose class I wrote several terrible stories. The one I remember best, in mortifying detail, was called "Cadillac," a story about a woman with no discernible personality who decided to steal a car for no discernible reason. Her name was Carla. The professor hated everything I wrote and suggested several times that I give up. I was a prodigy at nothing except stubbornness: He tried to discourage me, and I decided to spite him. I am stubborn, you are pertinacious, she is a vengeful untalented banshee—but a published one.

(Sometimes I think of those high school theater teach-ers who saw me try out again and again, and I wonder:

Would it have hurt to give me a part? Those plays were full of terrible actors, by which I mean teenagers. Given the chance to act, I might have learned. Maybe they sensed that I would never truly be part of a joint enterprise; maybe high school is when I forsook all group activities and swore off crowds and collaborators. Mostly, I'm grateful. I never longed to act, because I never knew what it felt like. I took a later, wonderful fiction teacher's advice and got some emotion into my writing, but it took a while to manage real longing and pain—the usual terror of being known, possibly why I was such a terrible actress. Then life worked me over and I did.)

In the center of the oval car was an oval bench. Around the edge of the car, a railing. I took a spot at the rail facing inward, toward the spokes of the Eye. A small girl joined me. Two years old perhaps, dark-haired, with the kind of round gut that pushed her T-shirt out so that you could see the ventral curve of her tummy, a look seen on toddlers and beer-drinking men. The T-shirt was pale yellow and said in white lettering, *BOBO'S 80!!!* You had to strain to see.

"Mim," said a similarly dark-haired man, sitting on the bench in the center. He slapped his flank. "Mim!" Mim ignored him and put one hand at the crook of my knee. *Dear Mim,* I thought, *you may stay.* I smiled at the man, whose pale-blue shirt said, in white lettering, *BOBO'S 80!!!* In fact, every person in the capsule wore a T-shirt that said *BOBO'S 80!!!* with one exception: an upright old woman with steel-gray hair, whose T-shirt had her own photograph printed upon it and, below, *I'M 80*. No exclamation points. Bobo herself. She was smiling in the photo. She was not smiling on the London Eye. Of course, I was an exception, too.

Bobo's descendants fanned out in the capsule. A pack of brunettes, muttering in English. I couldn't tell what sort of accent they had. Bobo herself sat in the middle of the capsule. Her purse was in her lap. She endured the turning and the height for the sake of her family and glared at me, the party-crasher.

"I'm sorry," said the man who'd called Mim's name.

"She's fine," I said, but then Mim took her hand away and I was left looking out at the city alone. The standing members of the family had gone to the outer edge of the capsule to look downriver. I'd chosen the inward view so that I could look at the other points of the clock, up, up, till we crested and came around the other side and everyone would see that I had positioned myself in the best place, staring upriver at the more famous parts of London.

We stopped. The whole apparatus. The entire London Eye. I looked down at the platform to see a man who walked with what my mother would have called Kenny sticks, those canes with cuffs around the forearms. Her own canes had right-angle handles. Fritz handles, a cane maker would say. The man boarded. In a joltless moment, we started moving again. The jolt was internal. I realized my mother could have gone on the London Eye: She could have driven her scooter right on. I had failed to know this and so I had failed to take her.

Was *this* grief? I could feel my mother's joy on the London Eye, her love of heights and good views. That streak of daredevilry and thrill-seeking. I had once taken her on a helicopter tour of downtown Miami, after she'd seen somebody parasailing and had guessed aloud that she couldn't do that. My mother laughed as the helicopter wove through skyscrapers; I believed I would fall to the ground at any moment and thought, *I've had nightmares like this.* That was actual joy; the joy I could apprehend now had not occurred, was counterfeit, made of regret and set in regret.

I stared down into the next capsule, at the teenagers with their green knapsacks, the cheap nylon kind with straps of black braid. Some of the kids sat on the floor and looked at their smartphones. A scruff-bearded man, a teacher, gestured toward all of London, *you should look,* and a girl shook her head and began to sort through a pack of cards. I wasn't afraid of heights, but I was afraid of a lot of things.

I am private; you are guarded; she will steal anyone's story, throw anyone to the sharks for the sake of a book.

No matter where you went, the view was of other people. Each capsule on the London Eye was filled with humanity, a diorama, a panel from a comic strip, an epic painting. Focus your brain and see it: capsule 15, the

Last Supper, Jesus in the middle, the apostles arranged around him, stunned, blaming themselves, *Is it me, Lord, is it me?* I wasn't sure whether the apostles said that in the actual Bible; I only knew the line as part of a joke somebody had once told me. Capsule 21, the Rape of the Sabine Women. Capsule 26, a man sawing a lady in half. You might see anything. A murder. An assignation. Either, at two ends of the same capsule. Thirty-two terrariums, numbered 1 through 12, 14 through 33. Display cases for the seabirds of the Thames. How people lived in the past. What people get up to now. I thought, *You should write a story that takes place on a Ferris wheel.* This was the sort of useless note I might find on a scrap of paper in my pocket, severed from inspiration, a bad fortune I'd given myself.

Mim touched the crook of my knee again, and her father leaned on the rail next to her. He wore rectangular metal-framed glasses, a rectangular birthmark high up on his cheek half-magnified by a lens. "They like you," he said. "Children."

"And why *not*?" I said heartily, playing the part of the uninvited guest. "Happy birthday to Bobo."

"Ha," he said, as though correcting me. "My grandmother." One of those families packing as many generations into a span of time as possible. I tried to do the math in my head. If Bobo is eighty (she *is* eighty) and this fellow is thirty, then . . .

It wasn't shocking. Only the sluggish reproduction of

my own family was. "Their great-grandmother," he said, gesturing to Mim and another child—the same size, same everything.

Twins. I said it: "Twins."

"Yes, twins."

"My mother was a twin," I told the righthand twin, Mim, in her yellow T-shirt. Her sister was in a green T-shirt. My mother loved seeing twins out in the world, insisted on telling them, "You know, I'm a twin, too," even though the children must have thought it was a lie: She was an old lady, all alone. The children didn't realize that one day their twinhood would be invisible, because each would mostly or entirely go out in the world without the other.

"Ah!" said the man. "And were they happy, the twins of your family?"

I told the truth. "Yes and no."

Then we were at the top of the London Eye. Then we headed down. It was boring. We were in a waiting room, waiting to be returned to the world, changed because we hadn't been changed and were disappointed. I angled myself toward the door to be the first to disembark. I didn't want to get caught up. I didn't want to wait. I didn't give Bobo a second look.

I produced a single worthwhile short story in college, my last semester, for a class taught by that brilliant woman who suggested I write about people with emotions. It was about a girl and her difficult mother, a mother who didn't resemble mine, except a little in the first sentence, but when I read it aloud at an event at my university, which was also my mother's place of work, she was at the back of the room, and every time I said the words *my mother*, a few more people—her co-workers, my friends—turned to look at her. My mother. My flesh-and-blood mother, who cannot be represented in any autobiographical or fictional or autofictional prose, not even this sentence I'm currently typing. I don't write autofiction. I don't even know what it is, though it sounds like it might be written by a robot, or a kiosk, or a European.

Did all those eyes make my mother feel self-conscious? No: famous.

That my mother and I had been able go to London together was astonishing. Truly astonishing. Though *astonishing* is one of my favorite words, all my uses of it pale compared to this, my mother, entirely herself, in 2016, after the terrible American election, before the cataclysmic inauguration, eating hot chestnuts from a Christmas market in front of Tate Modern.

In September 2011, her ordinary perambulation had slowed. She required a walker; then—she couldn't walk at all. She called her walking *perambulation*, which got at both the complexity of it and also made it sound non-medical, even humorous. All her life her body had been variously stiff. She decided at last to get the spinal surgery her orthopedist had been suggesting for years, two

vertebrae fused in her neck. She'd put it off partly because she was terrified that the doctors would shave her
head, though she also disliked orthopedic surgeons as a
class of people. They saw her body as a puzzle they could
solve. They made grand promises, and the results were
equivocal; she'd acquired her first pair of canes while recovering from surgery on her hips and needed them ever
after. My father—alive in 2011—hated hospitals the way
some people do, with a religious conviction they believe
sets them apart. My mother liked to spare him, so I flew
out for the operation. As long as I was in town, my father didn't have to worry about the length of his hospital
visits. He and I shared healthcare-proxy duties for my
mother. I knew the most important directive: Preserve
the hair.

The surgical waiting room was a windowless place
with a phone on one wall and on another a TV that always seemed to be showing reruns of *House*, a body passing through the MRI machine like a gondola beneath a
Venetian bridge. I read a book. Every fifteen minutes,
like a figure on a mechanical clock, I snapped the book
shut and wondered, *What is taking so long?*

Finally, the surgeon came to talk to me. He looked
shaken. Awful to see a shaken surgeon. A pen had burst
in the pocket of the lab coat he must have just put on, a
royal-blue Rorschach. "More damage than we thought,"
he said. "Was she ever in some kind of a car accident?
Years ago, maybe."

"Not that I know of."

"We fixed it. I think we fixed it."

Soon my mother was in recovery, and I brought her the thing she insisted she'd want as soon as she was conscious: a chopped-liver sandwich from Rubin's Delicatessen. This sandwich delighted and revolted the surgical ICU team. "You can't eat that!" a nurse said. "Your neck is all swollen."

"Delicious," my mother proclaimed, and took a bite, and swallowed it down. "Thanks, ducks," she said to me.

I said, "The surgeon wondered whether you'd been in an accident. Like, decades ago."

She regarded her sandwich, which would have been startlingly large for such a small senior citizen even had she not been propped up in a hospital bed recovering from spinal surgery. "Dodge-'em cars," she concluded.

"I beg your pardon?"

"At the Iowa State Fair. When I was a teenager. I snapped my neck back and couldn't move it for weeks."

That night my father and I went out to celebrate the indomitable spirit and body of my mother. We ate oysters and toasted her. *La Signora,* we called her, because once we'd all been in Florence together and in my halting Italian I'd asked a young guard outside the Uffizi if my mother could skip the line, and when he saw her he'd said, *"Ah! Per la signora? Certo, certo!"* and let us in.

Two days later, I flew back to Texas. The day after that, my father called: Something had gone wrong. My mother needed brain surgery. By the time I got back to Boston, my mother was unconscious, a patch above her hairline shaved to accommodate a ventricular tube, slurping away fluid. (My memory has added *slurping*. The tube was silent, an ordinary drain. I don't know why the slurping comforts me.)

That was the start of a long bad time. She picked up a bowel infection, which made her confused. Medically confused, I mean, as though brain-damaged, able to say only a handful of words. *Let's go. Let's get out of here. Let's go home.*

"At this age, nearly everything manifests as confusion," one kind doctor told me. He was tall and bald, with a wrinkly puppyish forehead. "She might recover, though with a patient like this"—he looked at my tiny elderly mother, semi-conscious in her bed—"Things can fall apart very quickly."

I'd known she might die, and I'd hoped she wouldn't. Hearing both possibilities expressed as a medical opinion made it seem inconceivable that she'd ever get better. (I lacked imagination. I still do. It's a common failing in my line of work.) I reconciled myself to her impending death. My hospital-hating father came to visit often but couldn't bear to sit for long by her side, and my mother wouldn't have wanted him to: When he was in the hospital after he'd had a heart attack in his fifties, she, too, had alighted and left. I stayed with my mother and at the end of the day picked my father up for dinner somewhere nice, with a wine list, and we would talk—about history but also about family. He was a fond, foolish old man.

Somehow I, the child of two people not particularly motivated by guilt, was consumed by it. It was as though I believed a stranger was keeping track of the hours I stayed by my mother's bed. The nurses, maybe. God, who I did not believe in. Maybe it was my maternal grandmother's guilt skipping a generation and landing hard, fully manifesting.

Those days were a dress rehearsal for my mother's easy actual death seven years later. I came to accept that it was possible; I pondered some hard decisions I thought I would have to make once and imminently. I believed I understood the story I was in: My mother was about to die. But the story kept shifting and I couldn't follow. I can't remember how many days I stayed there; I wish I'd kept a diary or taken notes. Later, the second time, I did.

"Let's go home," she said in 2011. "Let's get out of here." Every time it was as though she'd just had that thought. It was the only thing she said—I was about to say *for weeks,* but it might have been a bad twenty-four hours. My mother was one of those people who looked completely different when she smiled than when she was serious. Smiling involved all the muscles of her face. Her high cheekbones narrowed her eyes, and she showed her large, cantilevered teeth. She wasn't photogenic: "Another damn picture with my eyes closed," she'd say. That is, she was smiling in it. My mother was nearly always smiling, a broad, beaming smile. *Radiant,* a friend of hers called it.

Serious, as she was in the hospital, her eyes seemed twice the size. The expressiveness of her eyebrows, always considerable, was one of the first things that returned to her. I could feel the effort she put into looking at me. "Let's get out of here," she said, with her persuading look. I thought of those words as light on the lake of her thoughts—she could say them because they were on the surface, but there was plenty beneath, palpable to her, irretrievable by me. If it had been a stranger in that bed, I might have guessed at them. But my mother's thoughts were her own and I didn't dare try.

My mother was capable of no sudden moves with her arms or her legs or anything below her neck, even under ordinary circumstances. Only her wit and her laugh were quick. She stretched her hand out to me in slow motion, curved, her index finger forward. She might have been pointing at me. *You, you're the one who can drive the getaway car.*

I took her hand. I did this without permission. My mother was not a hand-holder. I sat by her bed. I said, "I'm sorry this happened to you." Without permission. I found her dear in her reduced state. I called her *honey.* I kissed her hello and goodbye. I can't imagine she approved of any of it.

Not this, either: typing sentences about her, calling her only *my mother,* as though that were her most important identity. "I don't approve," she said, of Barbie dolls, and certain flavors of bagels, and all bagels cut in half, and eating anything but the traditional pies on Thanksgiving; she disapproved of fiction written specifically for young adults (she believed they should be reading William Saroyan) and tutus on small girls. She enjoyed being a crank.

In the hospital I held her hand, and then I picked up the copy of *Peter Pan* I'd brought because I had a hard time making conversation with somebody unable to converse and because it was one of her favorite books. My father delivered monologues about Grover Cleveland and George V; my mother in her better days (I didn't know that she had plenty of better days ahead of her) spoke about herself and her family. I mostly was a conversational receptacle for my parents. I don't mean they weren't interested in me. They loved me, enjoyed my company, but on some fundamental level I'm not sure my mother, anyhow, cared about my inner life. This was a parenting gambit: Therefore I was allowed to do, think, whatever I wanted. She didn't (as Mrs. Darling does in *Peter Pan*) go into my mind to tidy things up, to hide the bad thoughts and plump up the good. The notion would have horrified her. She left my mind alone.

She loved *Peter Pan*. If she'd been herself, hearing me read aloud at her bedside, she would have thought, *I would do this so much better.* She would have told me so. She believed herself the best reader in any room; she'd been a speech teacher, among other things. I kept reading, partly to inflame her, to appeal to her pride—pride was one of her most developed organs; it pulsed away, surely—and partly because I thought, *If she dies, I don't want to look back at these days and see myself sitting dumbly by, checking my email.* I had my own pride; I was a theater person after all. It was a bit of stagecraft for the nurses and any other visitor who might stop by. *Look at how that woman loves her dying mother!*

After my mother's very slow and therefore particularly miraculous recovery, I asked her whether she remembered her hospital stay. Of course, she said. *Peter Pan?* No, not *Peter Pan.* This: One morning she had something very important to tell me. She labored at it, and I leaned in and asked her to repeat herself, one, two, three times, and then my father came into the room and I stood up and said joyously, "She says she wants to brush her teeth!"

She was moved from bed to bed, out of the ICU to the telemetry ward, where she was monitored from afar, upstairs in the hospital, downstairs. Because of the *C. diff,* the bowel infection, she was always in a private room, and anyone who went to see her needed to gown and glove up—PPE, I know to call it now—not so much so the hospital staff wouldn't catch it themselves but so they wouldn't spread it from room to room. It was easy to spread *C. diff* in a hospital. That's how my mother had caught it. Soon enough the infection was mostly what was wrong with her, along with its side effect, the persistent confusion.

I went home to Texas and worried about her hair. I'd stepped away and some surgeon had taken a hank, right at the front, where it was most noticeable. I bought wraps and turbans, though my mother, with her thick hair and her big noggin (another odd physical attribute of which she was proud), had never gone in for headgear. A friend of mine with curly hair had a genius hairstylist; when my mother landed in a nursing home near his salon, I tried and failed to arrange an appointment with him. My mother had to make do with the nursing home's beauty parlor, where every old lady got the same haircut, as though from a military barber. If my mother returned to herself, she'd be furious. The *C. diff* worsened, and she went back to the hospital. It got better and she was sent to a new nursing home. My father and I didn't understand how it happened, this sideways incarceration. We'd imagined you couldn't end up in a nursing home by mistake; you'd have to be signed over by a malicious child or an overwhelmed spouse. You couldn't just be sent there like a library book to a branch. My mother logged time in four or five nursing homes over those months, sent wherever there was space. We thought we should make a decision but didn't know how. More than once I asked my father if he wanted me to call the social workers or fly back to accost them in person, demand her release. He always said no. He was a grown-up and, moreover, frightened of the social workers, who had talked about making a home visit to see if the house was ready to receive my mother. The house wasn't ready to receive an able-bodied iguana, never mind a frail human woman, and my father didn't want a social worker making that determination.

Then the worst thing happened, which is that my mother got well enough to understand some of what had happened to her and called me, asking me to spring her. One day she left a very long message on my voicemail, audio of her talking to a nurse. My mother was begging to be let out of bed. She knew the longer she lay down, the harder it would be to ever walk again. The nurse berated her. Didn't my mother know she wasn't the only person in the world? Couldn't she understand she would just have to wait?

So I did call the social worker, who told me that we could have a family meeting to discuss it. Then my mother got shipped out of that nursing home and sent to the hospital and then back to a different nursing home.

I can't remember what we'd said to her friends. She'd mostly not told anybody about the surgery that led to this catastrophe. She had intended to recover quickly.

From this distance now, those days seem a chronological kink, science-fictional. My mother died (she almost died; she could have died). Then time ran backward, and she lived. I watched two versions of my mother's final illness, years apart. Three, if you count the one in reverse.

On the brink of death, emergency brain surgery, unconscious, conscious but incommunicative, communicative but nonsensical, communicative but with no knowledge of where she was, a mimeographed version of herself, out of the hospital and into a nursing home, herself but given to grudges and fury (which is to say not herself), herself but visibly depressed (ditto), herself in every way but mobility, back at home with twenty-four-hour-a-day help, back at home with daily help. Finally, astoundingly, back at home in charge of her life for years. She celebrated her eightieth birthday in New York at Katz's Deli with another chopped-liver sandwich, though by then she was a widow. My father had had his second, fatal heart attack a year and a half before. (I miss him. I'm sorry he doesn't fit in this book. I'm sorry his last year was unhappy.)

And my mother *did* go to the genius hairstylist, a tall funny man who'd been a guitarist and still had an eighties' rock-and-roll glamour. She went not just once but regularly. I took her to his postage-stamp salon two days after my father's death. She didn't mention anything till the genius hairstylist asked after him. "He died," my mother said. The hairstylist stopped cutting and said, "No *shit*?" "Yup," said my mother. The man shook his head, touched my mother's hair, and resumed his work. My mother loved that story. It was how she thought you should think about death. You swear with surprise and then you go on.

After my father's memorial service a month later, I told

my mother I could stay a few days and help get some things straightened out, or I could rent a car and we could go to New York.

We spent two nights, saw three Broadway shows, went to four museums, saw ten relatives. My mother is the one who kept score. *Let's go*, she had said. *Let's get out of here.* For the next few years, we did.

Her new short hair was magnificent, thick and wavy, a few black strands among the white. Eccentric and striking and wild. She was as vain about it as she ever was. Why had she waited so long?

Everyone knows that it's noble to go to museums unaccompanied. Look at us solitary exhibition gawkers: We pause to read the captions, we wander the rooms at a thoughtful speed, we think things, and therefore we're allowed to drink early and often.

Not *too* early. By the time I got to Tate Modern, it was 10:30 A.M., and I took the elevator to the restaurant at the top of the front building. It wasn't open, but the bar was. I stood in line as everyone ahead of me ordered coffees— flat white, cappuccino, drip. The man behind the bar was as light blond as the gravel-voiced girl from the Inclinator. Eastern European, I thought, worried about his future in what was still at that moment Western Europe. He gave me the particular encouragingly impatient nod of a handsome man in food service. I tried to look as though I'd been planning to ask for a cup of coffee but had just now changed my mind, possibly for medical reasons.

"Do you have . . . a sparkling wine?" I asked.

"Prosecco, yeah," he said.

"Yes, please."

It's noble to go to museums and museum cafés alone, because other people, the ones in couples or groups, behave so terribly in them. Four or five people behind me in line had sent scouts out to secure seats, so that I, poor single museumgoer, here for the *art,* had to turn with my solitary glass of prosecco to see nowhere to sit. Finally I found a spot, a barstool at a counter by the plate-glass windows that looked onto the Thames and St. Paul's. I am a short person, like my mother before me, and old, and stout, too short to ride most bicycles meant for adults, too short to reach things off the top shelves in grocery stores, and too short to throw a flank onto a barstool and sit upon it. My mother raised me to be proud of my height in the way other parents raise children to be proud of their heritage. I would attend a parade of shortness, if there was such a thing. Still, sometimes, as with this barstool, it was a nuisance. I would have to scale the damn thing. Dreadful. I tried to surrender my dignity. *I didn't know you had any left,* I could hear my mother say, she who loved jokes at my expense. I prepared to clamber. The physics of it seemed impossible. I had to make winches and pulleys out of my own anatomy. At every moment I thought I'd fail. But then it worked and I was up and everything was fine again. It was the first time I'd sat since striding out that morning. The prosecco was cold and the view of London in the sun beauteous and I was separated from a chic septuagenarian couple by a pillar to my right, though I could see them between pillar and window as they leaned over their breakfast. They drank from espresso cups with diminutive handles they pinched between thumb and forefinger. I drank early in honor of my mother, who had no rules for drinking and delighted in a 9:00 A.M. airport margarita and never, in my experience, drank to excess. (My father did. My father could have used some rules.) One glass was plenty. My brain felt made of prosecco itself.

Once somebody is dead, the world reveals all the things they might have enjoyed if they weren't. My mother was a great appreciator. It was a pleasure to take her places, because she enjoyed herself so much and so audibly. That was her form of gratitude. When I took my mother to New York after my father's death, I asked her whether we should get the expensive hotel room, the pricey tickets to *The Book of Mormon*. "Let's!" she said, but she didn't mean *let's*, because at our first meal she explained that she would not be paying a penny on the trip: My father had left her in financial difficulty. (This turned out not to be the case; he left her in extreme financial confusion.) The announcement released her from both paying and thanking. When we were together in the following years, she picked up nearly no checks, and I was happy to pay and often waited bitterly for thanks that wouldn't come. Now I can see this quirk of my mother's as narratively significant. From her earliest childhood, she was treated as helpless when she knew she was not. She was a force of nature. The body that might have made her look weak to a stranger was the result of enormous physical strength and bloody-mindedness. The question of money made her feel weak. She wouldn't acknowledge that I was paying for everything, because she felt that it pointed out that she could not. (She could, but she didn't understand that.)

One of the reasons we had such a good time in London together is that I had decided to accept this, to take great pleasure in spoiling her and great pleasure in her company, because my mother—this is only true—was more fun than anyone I knew. She loved being alive and in the world; being alive and in the world with her was like dancing with someone who really knew how to lead. Out of my own vanity I'd hoped she would brag like the Jewish mother she was about how her daughter had spoiled her, but my mother was not a natural kveller. In graduate school, I was shocked to meet people whose parents didn't approve of them studying creative writing. My parents disapproved of very little that I did. They didn't approve, either: Whatever opinions they had about what I did, they kept to themselves. They believed my life was my own business. This, I understand now, is a great gift, though a gift that comes without kvelling.

She paid what was for her the greater compliment: She talked about what a good time we had together. On our trip to London, my mother and I had come to Tate Modern and passed beneath a Louise Bourgeois spider. I wasn't moving in our footsteps—my footsteps, her tire tracks—but I wasn't avoiding them. The exhibitions would be different, anyhow. I took the elevator down to the floor of the Tate's vast Turbine Hall and took the escalator up to the galleries; the second escalator dropped me off at a wall that said, NAN GOLDIN. *I know her,* I thought happily. I meant I knew her work. Outside the gallery, a sign said, CAUTION. VERY GRAPHIC IMAGERY.

The Goldin exhibition came in two pieces: a gallery of framed photographs and a darkened room featuring a slideshow of part of her magnum opus, *The Ballad of Sexual Dependency,* set to music Goldin had chosen. Did I really know her work? I'd seen it only in books and magazines. But I could hear the Velvet Underground coming from the darkened room, a song important to me, the drummer Moe Tucker singing, *"If you close the door/the night could last forever."* I followed the music into the dark, which was such that it took me a moment to see the seating, the merest gleam from the projected photos off the edge of a leather banquette. Nobody else was here. Decades-old squalor and glamour on the screen: How many of these people were still alive? Here in my own time, they were projected on a museum wall, where they smoked and shot up and fucked, glitter-eyed and full of longing. The mattresses were bare, or in hotel rooms. Here's a hotel bed made up. Here it is, hours later, roughed around, no people but the insinuation of bodies in bedclothes. *Bedclothes:* what a beautiful, mysterious word. No other furniture wears clothing. The same handsome man from a photo seven back. A family album of people who'd been estranged from their families. Bruised, drugged. Not misspent youth: Here they were, inside a museum.

Here I was, too. Here I am. Passing for ordinary, but I am not ordinary. I am not normal. The opposite of ordinary is not extraordinary; the opposite of ordinary is dozens of words that have nothing in common with one another.

I felt—and I feel, as I put together these sentences— that when you become a flaneur or a flaneuse, you are supposed to disappear from the narrative. (Same thing when you are a mother.) You're an everyperson. An ascetic in the personality department. The city is a coat you're wearing. Who cares about the shape beneath, when the shape is changed by the wind as you walk, by each turn of the weather.

No, no, I don't wanna. I packed my personality and my sense of humor in order to peregrinate.

The Goldin slideshow ended, but I'd joined in the middle and hadn't seen it all. Dedicated to her sister. *In memory of*—a list of too many names to read. I obeyed Maureen Tucker. I forsook the light and waited for the start, for more.

Other people came into the room. In a traditional slideshow—*let's learn how our medieval ancestors baked bread in the house*—people sit, but for *The Ballad of Sexual Dependency* most of the people lurked at the door. They'd been warned that some of the imagery was VERY GRAPHIC. They didn't want to seem as though they were enjoying it. Two men took the banquette next to me. One of them was not quite grown, a teenager. They began to speak French in low tones. Would I shush them? I'm a committed shusher. I used to be a public librarian, a job in which I didn't actually shush anyone. Used to be. Not anymore. A friend once told me how important it was to know in fiction what people do for a living, how they made their money. Why do I always want to dodge the question? For some years I have made my living (what a curious turn of phrase) as a teacher of creative writing. I claim to like it. I suppose I do. That is, I enjoy reading other people's work and having opinions.

Can writing be taught? Not by me.

The Francophone boy got out his telephone and consulted it, in this new world in which nearby strangers may invade your reveries through multiple senses with technology. He was too far away for me to nudge or finger wag, though this is something I would do in a theater. He put away his phone. On the wall: a large monochromatic erection. I don't know how it is for men: Is a portrait of an erection always about somebody else, or about you, or about somebody else and therefore about you? To me it seemed a harebrained interrogating object. The boy got up and left, and soon thereafter his companion followed.

After the slideshow I was full of thoughts and ambition, as I always am in museums. To be surrounded by years of other people's work—I needed to write things down, so I went back to the gift shop at the bottom of the museum to get a notebook and a pen. *You're a writer: Don't you always have a pen and paper?* I mean to. Things fall away from me. I don't know how. I own an encyclopedia's worth of notebooks, each purchased at a moment I feel full of inspiration, each filled for five pages and put aside. When I read them at a later date, it's like spirit writing: illegible (my handwriting is terrible), gnomic (*haunted by an abandoned hour,* I write, *hour* underlined three times), useless. Future scholars will be mystified and misled by these volumes, should an archive buy my papers, which is unlikely. I send all my papers to the Harry Ransom Center. The Harry Ransom Center is what I call my recycling bin. You can get good notebooks in gift shops but rarely good pens. At the Tate, I got a ballpoint pen and hated it. The most wonderful arguments among writers concern punctuation and stationery supplies. On these subjects, people say what they mean, regardless of other people's feelings or current mores. If you don't like semicolons, you cannot be persuaded to use one. It would be like wearing somebody else's underclothes. You may even encounter semicolons in another's work and despise them, as you would a mouse in somebody else's pantry.

There is something wrong with a person who loves ballpoint pens. I believe nothing so deeply as this.

I went to wander the galleries, worried about how abstract the rest of the art would be, because I am at root a philistine. A literalist. I want people in my art. Faces, yes, but also bottoms and elbows and any other part—that interrogative erection, or Nan Goldin's thigh with a heart-shaped bruise after her lover beat her. She photographed herself, the bruise in one picture, her battered face with blood in her eye in another, so she wouldn't go back to him. Hard to look at. I had looked at it awhile.

I found myself in a gallery dominated by a length of rope that ran down the wall and across the floor. A man in a black Utilikilt and a green T-shirt regarded it—indeed, it seemed the kind of art a Utilikilter might admire, practical on the surface but meaningless underneath. In the silence of the gallery, the man farted. I didn't laugh, because I was not standing next to someone I loved.

In a darkened room of Rothkos, another solitary man sat and peered into the phone in his lap. "Is it Persian?" he asked the person on the other end of the line, except no line, the person either elsewhere in London or a continent away. "You can turn the label over and see how many stitches per inch." *This isn't your phone booth,* I wanted to say. The Rothkos were floor-to-ceiling. In Houston, Texas, a couple of hours from where I lived, there was a famous chapel full of Rothkos. Rothko famously killed himself. In the presence of enormous Rothkos, you were meant to be silent, to think about death and color and the great man, and yet here was an ungreat man discussing rugs. I hated him with no more hatred than I had for all people using their phones in irritating ways, which is to say—have you been paying attention?—instantaneously and all-consumingly, the kind of hatred other people reserve for fellow citizens visibly of other religions. A moral loathing. The dimwits checking their bright messages mid-movie, the sociopaths on speakerphones in airports, the ambling ninnies slowing down to peer at the news, even the more sociable chuckleheads taking photographs of beloveds on that picturesque bridge. Surely I have the right to pluck the phone away. Toss it in the water. Or bump their cars as they swerve and text. I want to call the police on them, and they will not be able to film me, my face contorted by hatred and judgment, because I will have already confiscated their phones.

Maybe it's necessary to hate categories of people, because it's too much to assume that everyone has a soul. You would be clobbered and hobbled by the knowledge. And so each of us strikes categories off the list, and the question is where you draw the line. Saints, maybe, never do. Myself, I don't wish to care about men who wear their hair long and then slick it back so you can see the comb marks, for instance. The man jabbering amid the Rothkos was such a one.

In the Rothko room I judgmentally sat on the bench and assumed an expression of great contemplation and sorrow aimed inward but also directly at the throat of the man with the phone: *You there, cretin, I am thinking about death.* (I was not thinking about death, not even my mother's.) Into his lap the man said, "You wanna see a Matisse? Let's go," and carried his phone and therefore his auditor to cheerier climes, leaving me in the dim light, surrounded by enormous Rothkos, which, I realized, meant not a thing to me, and never had. Abstract art. I hate it.

If, despite everything, I began work on a memoir and wrote down everything I remember for sure about my life—all of my life—I might be able to assemble a pamphlet. If I wrote down everything I know about fiction: a second, smaller pamphlet. What I believe: It makes a difference how tall people are, how short, how much they weigh. How they move; how it feels to be them, temperature, hips, itch, swoon. Young writers sometimes catalog every thought and emotion of a character without knowing their weight or their gestures. But if you don't take your characters' bodies into account, your work is in danger of being populated by sentient, anguished helium balloons. I tell my students all the time, *Don't forget your characters' physical selves.* If your characters feel distant, remember their specific gravity on the earth. If you know what a character is doing with her hands, you might know what she's doing with her head. If you know her feet, you may know her soul.

About my mother's feet, I could write volumes. They were very short, in the odd no-man's-land between children's shoes and women's. I still don't know why this gap exists: Most people who live to adulthood have feet this size at some point. Is it because teenagers grow so quickly, and why make shoes meant for a week of wear? Is it that if your feet are this size only passingly during adolescence, you're likely wearing sneakers anyhow? *Sneakers* is what my mother called them, so I do, too, though I was raised among people who called them tennis shoes, or tennies.

My mother's feet were wide, triple E's, with a very high instep, and also flat. "My feet are square," she sometimes said. Officially, quantitatively, they were probably size four (right) and three and a half (left), though the measurement is academic, since my mother never wore shoes that fit her. She generally bought shoes that would merely stay on. I don't know how many pairs of shoes she owned. Hundreds, seemingly, mostly children's, enough for all the orphanages of the world.

I might have grown into a woman who complained about how hard it was to buy shoes for my own peculiar feet—wide, flat, unfit for pumps and stilettos and the womanly shoes available in any store—but I grew up going to shoe stores with my mother. I complained of having no shoes until I met a man with no feet—though this is nonsensical, both of you were missing something that might have made your life easier. Anyhow, the man with no feet doesn't need your pity. Or shoes, for that matter. My mother, the child of shopkeepers, liked having her feet measured and marveled at, her foot on the podiatric slide rule, the salesman on the vinyl stool with the slanted-front footrest. In those days, it seems to me, it was mostly men who sold women's shoes. Why is that? Something scientific to it, I guess. Or romantic. To tell the truth, I think my mother missed fluoroscopes, those dilettante's x-ray machines once found in shoe departments, including the one in her parents' store. She liked the crouching salesman—perhaps sales*men* for the theater and quotidian kink of it—scratching the back of his head as he thought and said, "Would you wear a little boy's oxford?"

As long as they were natty, she would.

We stopped anywhere that might have shoes to fit her, children's shops and large department stores. No orthopedic specialists, no place that also sold walking sticks and compression socks. My mother had spent her childhood wearing shoes with good support; good support, whether at the ankle or the bustline, was something my mother's mother believed in and my mother herself renounced. My grandmother had earned, besides her JD, her GC: Graduate Corsetiere. That is, she was trained to fit girdles and brassieres and liked, to my great discomfort, to sit next to me on a bench at the Merle Hay Mall in Des Moines, Iowa, and mutter what underwear passing women would look better in.

We were on that bench because I lived in Iowa, too, eventually, and my grandmother was trying to educate me. It was 1988. I'd applied to three MFA programs in both fiction and poetry; in those days I wrote poetry more seriously than fiction. I was accepted in poetry by one program but offered no financial support; was rejected in both from the second; and was offered a spot in fiction with a minuscule amount of money by the Iowa Writers' Workshop. (No holder of an MFA has forgotten their graduate school funding.) Every month I took a Greyhound bus from Iowa City to Des Moines to visit my grandmother, who was thrilled to have me close. She made me crash a bar mitzvah my first visit, and took me out to her supper club, and asked me when I was going to get married, and took me to card games and on senior-citizen bus trips to see the tulips in Pella, Iowa, and celebrations of Valley Junction, and showed me the family photo albums. I came to understand: Your family is the first novel that you know. How did that handsome boy become that blinking uncle? Who's this unexplained big-hatted lady? Before I lived in Iowa, I might not have been that interested in my mother. It's a tendency of the young to believe—to hope—that everything skips a generation. In Des Moines, I took notes. In Iowa City, I wrote stories about Des Moines and was occasionally told that my characters weren't believable, particularly the ones most like my relatives. I never wrote about my mother.

Would I be a different writer if I hadn't gotten my MFA? More original and unconstrained? Stubborner about my weaknesses and obsessions, as weird as I ever wanted to be, as strange as I still am? I wonder. On the other hand: Would I still be writing? Probably not. I gave up writing poetry when I didn't get into a poetry program, gave it up and didn't look back.

My mother needed so many shoes because of her mercurial feet. They swelled in humidity. The tendons seized up. In later years her muscles stopped cooperating and it became a struggle to get any shoes onto her feet. Somehow I forgot this until she visited me, or I visited her, and it was my job to shoe my mother. "Time to go!" I'd say, and she'd say cheerily, "OK, I need to get my shoes on." If all she brought were the cheap Keds lace-ups she favored, this could take half an hour. She owned dozens of pairs of Keds, which she insisted fit her. "Pull on the tongue," she'd command, as I knelt and toiled.

"They don't *fit*," I'd say, out of breath.

"Nobody else has this problem," she claimed. By *nobody* she meant the various aides who helped her around the house. I later pettily interrogated them. My mother, it pains me to say, it delights me, was lying.

In advance of one of her visits to Texas, I decided that even this problem could be solved by the internet. I spent hours. I wanted my mother attractively, durably, easily shod. The women's shoes started at size five; the children's shoes were sparkly purple or Dickensian. I discovered the word *adaptive* and the world seemed full of possibility. I ordered eleven pairs of adaptive shoes: oxfords with Velcro that opened flat so you basically origamied them onto a foot, cloth slippers that cost the earth, Mary Janes for children with spasticity. We tried them all and sent back the clunkers. "I love them," my mother said of the three pairs that fit, and then the next visit showed up with the same damn beige Keds and explained she was saving the shoes I'd got her for a special occasion.

At home she went barefoot, because at home she walked. In her old age she used a walker inside; when she was younger, she stuck her canes in the rack by the front door and did without, to work on her balance. She kept a cane in the bathroom, which she used as a hook to pull on clothing; even after she stopped using canes for perambulation, she always traveled with one as a useful tool. She used her bare feet as a kind of sense, to guard against falling—feet in shoes couldn't feel the slope of a threshold or know when they'd caught the edge of a carpet. My grandmother sent bedroom slippers to the whole family; as a child I disdained them because my mother did.

Out in the world, my mother fell. She fell in Lord & Taylor when the rubber tip of her cane hit a drop of water on the marble floor; a passing bodybuilder said, "May I?" and picked her up and set her on her feet like it was nothing, notable both because he asked permission and knew what he was doing; my mother was bedeviled by men who decided she needed assistance and tried, without asking, to carry her down flights of stairs. She fell at a resort in upstate New York at the top of a mountain, in her room, and the hotel doctor told her she was being a baby about the pain—she wasn't actually complaining, she just said she couldn't get up—and my father called an ambulance to take her off the mountain, and it turned out she'd dislocated her shoulder. She fell down the stairs of her sister's house and whacked her head—I was in the living room and saw—with such force I felt it ringing in my own cranium for weeks, would suddenly clutch my head in sympathy. She fell in the bathroom of a Greek restaurant and insisted my father drive her to meet me at the theater anyhow, a napkin full of ice held to her head; when she took it away, there was a streak of blood in her hair. She fell at home, too. Once, I arrived at the house to find her on the floor of the kitchen. "I lay down myself," she said. "I decided it would be easier to sleep here."

"That's not true," I said.

"It *is* true," said my mother, who had written this particular story. "Help me up."

(I've heard some memoirists say that they don't worry whether their renditions of people are "fair," since there is no *fair:* We all have our own memories, and a memoir is one person's. What's the difference between a novel and a memoir? I couldn't tell you. Permission to lie; permission to cast aside worries about plausibility. "Is your work autobiographical?" people like to ask, and when I was young I would say, "No, not factually, but it's emotionally autobiographical." I believed it. I hid things in my early stories, amid the circus performers and the elderly criminals, the drunks, the tattooed woman, the mysterious huckster who insisted she was family. I gave characters my secrets but not my face or biography; I saddled them with things I believed about myself but had never told anyone, a painter putting my face in a convex mirror at the back of the room, an engraver hiding my initials in the mane of a historical horse. I trembled at my own honesty; I was terrified that people would see the coded truth. Would I have wanted to be found? Not in a million years. Desperately. Now I don't give a fuck. Or I do, and I've just said that to throw you off the trail.)

My mother would admit to falling. "It's one of my talents," she said. She often sorted things into *one of my talents* or *not one of my talents*. If you fall, you need to relax into it. Go all the way down. Don't put out your hands: You'll break your wrists that way, and if you use canes, you need your wrists to walk. "Did you know, drunks don't hurt themselves when they fall," she told me. "Because they just fall, and then they're happy to be on the ground."

In this way I was better prepared than the offspring of formerly steady-on-their-feet elderly parents. What if she falls? She'll be all right. She always has been. She'll bounce right back. Besides, what was the alternative?

That was how my mother stayed alive: She walked. She always walked. Even when she came back from her time in nursing homes after the botched spinal surgery, after she'd been told she might not walk, shouldn't walk, it was with the certainty that she would walk again. She practiced and stretched every day, often with the aides. My mother had an excellent brain and a quick tongue and a lovely personality, but the most staggering thing about her was her will. If you have difficulty walking, strangers will tell you constantly that you shouldn't try.

When she moved through the world by foot and cane, porters in airports tried to talk her into a wheelchair. She never accepted. She knew that the moment a porter got her in a wheelchair, she would be turned to luggage. "It'll be faster," the porters would say. "I don't care," she'd answer. She drove people crazy. *You have made me notice you, and now I must solve you.* One of the reasons she loathed hospitals and nursing homes: Nobody would let her walk. "It's not safe," people would tell her. But it wasn't safe for her not to walk. "Let me get somebody to put you in a wheelchair," she might be told, but she wanted to move her own body. Not such a big thing to ask. Walking is what kept her alive, what allowed her to live at home, even when her husband had essentially given up walking himself, even when he died. The Little Engine That Could, if you don't remember, is a woman.

Her feet were so small and weird and dear. She got older. Stiffer. Couldn't reach them. Other people tended to her feet so her feet could keep her on the face of the earth. I'm not sure how long she was off them, before the surgery, during the long months of her incarceration, after she got home. I only know that in September 2011 she wasn't walking, and by the end of 2012 she was, and she continued to walk, every single day. She walked for six years more, as a matter of principle, and health, and independence, and necessity. "If I don't get up and walk, I'll ossify," she'd say. I can hear the sound of the soles of her bare feet on a wooden floor, *chsk, chsk, chsk.* The sound was always the same. It only ever got slower.

My father loved trains, and my mother took many to humor him, including, when they were in their mid-seventies, from Copenhagen to Prague, switching in Cologne. My father had gone ahead with the luggage while my mother walked alongside the cars, wondering how to board. She hadn't figured it out by the time the train pulled out of the station. Aboard, my father understood that my mother was on the platform, panicked, looked around, saw the emergency-stop cord, considered things for half a moment, and pulled. The train stopped; my mother was lofted by the hands of half a dozen Germans, *light as a feather*, and everyone involved agreed that this was a reasonable use of the passenger emergency brake.

"And was that a lifelong dream of yours, to pull the cord

for a good reason?" I asked when my father told me the story.

"Yes," he said quietly, moved to be so understood.

My mother preferred boats—wind and water, a panoramic view—and one of the blessings of the electric scooter of her later years was that boats became easier to board. I decided to take one in her honor, the ferry from one Tate (Modern) to the other (Britain). First I found a little grocery store and got myself a sandwich and a brownie and brought them to the counter, where a ponytailed young woman looked at me dubiously. I thought about buying cigarettes—I smoke sometimes when I travel—but they were kept behind doors, so you couldn't look at brands and then say casually, "Silk Cut, please." You had to be a serious smoker with a plan, and I wasn't. Years before I'd been a devotee of the English ten-pack; a lovely thing, to be able to buy just ten cigarettes at a time. Like my father before me, I fooled myself when it came to bad behavior. I worried that the young woman behind the store counter wouldn't like me if I asked. For any large thing, I don't worry about judgment. Only the cigarettes, the 10:30 A.M. prosecco. Only going on a Ferris wheel by myself, alone and middle-aged. She had a pretty, lupine face.

I pretended I didn't speak the language, put my sandwich and brownie on the counter, and paid in coins, which I counted out as though I were unfamiliar with the notion of money. I tried to look worthy of kindness.

"All right?" said the young woman behind the counter, running her dark ponytail through a loop of her thumb and forefinger.

I nodded.

The sandwich was marked *cheddar cheese and cress.* I wasn't sure what cress was—English and green, that was the sum of my knowledge—and the cheese appeared to have been prepared in some sort of salad, as in egg salad, or tuna, suspended in what might have been salad cream. (The least appetizing words in the world concern English food: *salad cream, baps, butties, carvery, goujons.*) I took a bite. It was a bad sandwich; I wrapped it back up in the plastic. I took a bite of the brownie, which was simultaneously oversweet and yet not sweet at all, sugary in patches of unflavored sand. This made me nostalgic for the sandwich, so I took a bite of that, which made me long for the brownie, and in this alternating way I finished both except a little elbow bend of sandwich crust.

A boat—a Thames Clipper, the line was called, though it didn't have sails—was pulling up, but nobody ahead of me was rushing, and I took my time down the ramp to the pier, only to see them already drawing in the tiny gangplank.

"I've just missed the boat to Tate Britain, haven't I?" I said to the woman on the dock as she hooked the security rope back in place.

She nodded and squinted at the electric timetable behind me. "Another in fourteen minutes."

So I sat on a damp bench and felt unlucky for several seconds in a row. Transportation mishaps always feel tied up in fate, not mere inconvenience: A missed boat is an ill omen indeed. Then I noticed I was sitting on the river in London, with a view of St. Paul's, and thought: *Who could feel unlucky in this setting?* My mother was casual about time, to say the least, and now I could see it as self-preservation. The physical world—by which I mean specifically the world constructed by able-bodied people for able-bodied people—conspired against her. On any given day, particularly when she walked everywhere, she might come up against dozens of obstacles. More than dozens. The small, usual ones; the bigger catastrophes. A broken elevator; a few stairs without a banister; an arrowed sign marked with that stick figure riding in a wheelchair, which meant that the entrance was level but miles away from where she intended to go. A tile floor on a rainy day that she could not cross by herself. A locked door. Once, her employer invited her to a meeting on campus accessibility—as my mother pointed out, it was telling that the university committee was called not "accessibility" but "compliance," meaning compliance with the Americans with Disabilities Act—and when she showed up, late, they told her that she was the first employee with a disability who'd come to one of the meetings, despite many invitations. She apologized for her lateness and explained that she'd had to crawl up the front stairs on her hands and knees to get there, because while there were elevators *inside* the building, there was no accessible entrance from the street.

The world got in her way, and in order to not be furious with the world, to love it with her optimist's heart, she decided, reasonably, that punctuality was not essential—though she insisted that she was never late if she could help it. She was casual about timeliness for everything but theater curtains. Then she was a stickler. But a missed boat when there was another boat in fourteen minutes was not a missed boat; it only meant you were early for the next one.

Here it came. A deckhand looped the mooring rope and threw it and missed and it landed in the water. The disappointment showed in his cheek as he hauled it up and felt the dampness of the river. The second time he made it. Every day he would have the experience of success and failure, and I wondered whether the pleasure of lassoing the mooring erased the letdown of missing it.

That's how it is with work, if you're lucky. *Write every day*, say some people, but not me, because I don't, and never have. I imagine it's satisfying advice to dispense, an instruction people can follow or not, good advice for people for whom it's good advice. I cannot do it. I need other ways to guard against laziness and procrastination. Any way you get work done is a good way to work. Times I didn't write: The year I lived in Philadelphia. September 1, 2006, through May 2, 2007. During the university semester while teaching in my twenties and thirties. Before and after my first novel was published. Mid-March to late August 2020. Weeks at a time, months.

Times I did write: After people died, almost instantly. In hospitals. Crying from a variety of heartbreaks. While working a forty-hour-a-week job as a librarian. At 3:00 A.M. staying up; at 5:00 A.M. getting up. Always in the face of failure. Not always in the face of success.

What doesn't kill you won't make you stronger, but at least you'll recognize its face on a WANTED poster.

Having missed a boat, I was first in line for the next. I went up the gangplank, followed by an armada of ladies pushing empty strollers and their admiralty of small boys who walked beside their transport.

It was warm for London. I found it sublime. The information board on the boat said it was twenty-five degrees. I tried the conversion an English friend had once given me: Double the number and add thirty. Eighty. Could that be right? Of all the theoretical superiorities of Europeans over Americans—the food, the free healthcare, the paid maternity leave, the lack of guns—the surest sign, I thought, was the ability to understand the nuances of such small differences in temperature. I believed this even though I also believed, like any American, that Fahrenheit was superior. Beautiful, even. There's not enough room in Celsius for beauty.

I put my face to the sun as we went out on the river. The small boys kept getting away from their mothers. "No, Cholly," said one mother. "Cholly. Come here." The day had been full of children, I realized, more visible because I was a motherless child and feeling it. Cholly was two years old and in trouble.

"*Cholls,*" said his mother. She snagged his wrist and settled him into his stroller and fastened all around him the lunatic's restraints. Then she turned to one of her friends, another young mother, and said with great certainty, "Swordfish."

I don't like eavesdropping. I prefer my own inane thoughts.

The first stop was Embankment, where several middle-aged puce-faced besuited men strode off; by *middle-aged* I realized with a shock that I meant *my age.* So I reflected with pleasure that *puce* came from the word *flea* and meant just that: the color of a flea. The next stop was Millbank, and Tate Britain. I had gone there on yet a different trip with my mother, when I'd been in my thirties and she in her sixties. This, I suddenly realized, was shortly after her own mother had died and she'd come into a little money, enough for a plane ticket. I hadn't forgotten that trip, but I had forgotten that it, too, was just after a mother's death. All the London visits of my life were layered over one another like posters pasted up on a city wall. As I went through the city, I experienced all of these trips at one time, sometimes worn away so I could clearly see the earliest one, sometimes quite thick so I could feel the buildup of travel, a kind of blurred, accumulated familiarity. I knew there was a fancy word for this effect—*palimpsest, pentimento*—but I am a child of the 1970s and I heard distant horns and thought, *8-track tape.*

The Thames Clipper pulled up at Tate Britain, which I had never before approached from the water. I disembarked and went up its steps. Most museums in London are free, gloriously, though they all have square Lucite boxes that suggest a donation. You'd think I'd donate money, to keep them free, but like my mother before me, I sometimes think if I'm too visibly grateful for a thing, people will think, *Yes, that is nice of us; your gratitude has made us realize, in fact, that it's so nice it's optional. Give it back!* I do my best instead to overspend in the gift shops and restaurants. On an ordinary day, I never would have bought myself a terrible cress-ridden sandwich—the sandwich is not my favorite food, I am un-American—but I had got it into my head that I would finish my day at the theater, as my mother would have liked, and now it was past one.

I knew where I was going. It was Mim of the London Eye and her sister—though then I realized I wasn't sure Mim's twin *was* a sister; then I realized I wasn't sure Mim herself was a sister, a herself. I'd only presumed. Mim and Mim's sibling, then—who'd put this idea in my head. I went to find one of my mother's favorite paintings: *The Cholmondeley Ladies,* pronounced *Chumley,* appropriate because they sat up chummily in bed next to each other, two identical women in lace, both holding angled swaddled babies as stiff as snowshoes.

The museum was arranged in chronological order. It didn't take long to find what I was looking for. There they were. Unknown painter; 1600s. As the caption on the wall noted, the Cholmondeley women weren't identical twins—their eyes were different colors—and perhaps not even fraternal. I had to look from one to the other, and the moment I stopped looking at one lady, I had already forgotten her particulars. In my head I described the differences in words. *Gray eyes, wider across the temple. Slightly taller. Weaker of chin.*

In this the Cholmondeley ladies were no different from anyone. I am terrible at faces. Not actually face-blind—I can learn faces. But I have to be able to look them over, and a haircut or new glasses or a hat turns even someone I know into a stranger. I have to meet somebody five times before I can reliably recognize them, and even then not always. War movies, in which everyone wears the same clothing and has the same haircut, are impossible for me to follow. If I study a face and commit it to memory— *almond-shaped eyes, a birthmark, distinctive teeth*—I have a hope of not embarrassing myself. Perhaps this is because my parents were so distinctive-looking. From childhood I didn't have to work to pick them out of a crowd.

Or perhaps I inherited this deficiency from my mother, who was even worse. Everyone recognized her:

the bun, the shortness, her very particular nose, her very particular smile, her posture, her canes, her dark eyebrows, which were like nobody else's, not even her twin sister's, who possessed much of what my mother did but subtler. Nothing about my mother's looks was subtle. How could she be expected to remember everyone who remembered her?

One Cholmondeley lady, then the other. One, the other. Her eyes farther apart. Her cheeks rosier. Did they resemble each other at all, or were they just making the same expression while dressed alike? They had two souls, without question, that old story, two souls and one bed. The more I looked, the more they seemed to be merely two white women put into matching outfits. Then I looked again and they were identical again.

I headed for the gift shop, where I could have bought a glass pitcher or a Warhol-inspired skateboard; a match safe with a picture of a seventeenth-century dandy; fridge magnets; a game to test your child's memory; neckties; plastic bento boxes; a beach ball; tea towels; lamps; blankets; baby clothing; a coloring book of great works of art; a set of false mustaches; tape measures; water bottles; windup toys; an anthology of postmortem photographs; a scarf printed with a map of World War II London; air fresheners; pushpins; coffee mugs; phone cases; dolls of great women; dolls of men who ordered the execution of their wives; salad tongs; cunning ice-cube trays (not cubes but handlebar mustaches); sleeping masks; necklaces made of old computer parts; freeze-dried ice cream; eyeglasses; sunglasses; decks of cards; satchels; nut-crackers; steak knives; corkscrews.

For the first time all day, I had a sense of my mother near me. She would meet me at any moment. She was just rolling through the later galleries; she loved the Pre-Raphaelites, especially Rossetti. Or she was here in the gift shop, digging through the sale table in the other room. I could see her. Not the old mother on the scooter but a younger self, standing up, holding both canes in one hand and turning things to read their prices with the other. I have a photograph of her at a flea market in What Cheer, Iowa, in this posture.

Was this the afterworld? My mother all by herself was a holiday, very good at buying presents and exceptional at receiving them. "Oh, you extravagant child!" she sometimes said to me, if I'd bought something she'd admired but thought too expensive. She took pleasure in presents not only because she liked things—things, that nearly fatal accumulation—but because she liked being thought of. A present, after all, meant just that: Out in the world, a person saw something and thought of you. The afterworld was made of the things I could not buy my mother, a charged net of things she could never possess. The things of the world.

I decided to try on the fancy reading glasses. In eye-sight, I took exactly after my mother, who was vain about her vision until she was forty-five, when the words in her book suddenly blurred. Me, too: When it happened, I blamed the medicine-bottle makers of the world for shrinking type, the frugal book designers who squeezed too much on a single page, an otherwise admirable student for printing out his thesis in the wrong font. My mother bought cheap gold-framed readers by the dozen from Amazon; she was always panicking that she didn't have glasses, when she had one pair in her hand and another on top of her head and half a dozen at the bottom of her bag. About reading glasses she had no vanity at all, though otherwise she loved accessories.

In the museum gift shop, I picked up a pair I thought were very Philip Johnson, though when I tried them on and looked in the mirror, I saw they were more Harry Potter. I tried on a pair of hot-pink glasses and laid my hand across my cheek and temple. I liked to fall asleep while wearing glasses—not just nod off while reading a book but purposefully, bespectacledly, close my eyes in bed and slide into dreams. It gave me a pleasant, blindered feel, a mild restraint that reminded me of something. I'd been—what, pigeon-toed?—a little askew in the legs when I was a child and for some time slept overnight in a pair of shoes attached to a bar to correct whatever was wrong. It occurs to me now that I can't find out what that was, since anyone who knew is dead. Hips? Legs? Knees? Feet? It doesn't matter. I never thought of it except when I put my feet on a support beneath a table, and then my feet remembered and pretended they couldn't move. It wasn't an unhappy memory. Perhaps sleeping with glasses reminded me, too.

But the hot-pink glasses made me look silly. Zany. I'd taken to coloring my hair, which was dark though not as dark as my mother's. When people referred to my hair as black, I always corrected them: My mother's hair was black; mine was darkest brown. Now my hair had russet highlights. I would not (as some of my country-women, middle-aged women across the globe) color parts of it blue or pink or fuchsia. *God keep me from zaniness*, I thought as I looked at myself in a pair of lime-green reading glasses. My mother sometimes tried on clothing in a store and asked, "Does this make me look like a crazy Cambridge lady?" By which she meant: too colorful, too bluey-purple, verging on high-end hippiewear, with a suggestion of bells sewn into the hem, Birkenstocks, comfort, *I just turned fifty and I don't care what other people think.*

I bought a pair of tortoiseshell glasses with tinted blue lenses. I thought they suited me, even though I knew I'd never see myself wearing them in the mirror again. I don't need glasses to see my own reflection.

"You never told me that your mother was a cripple," a seventh-grade friend once said to me, and I said, shocked, "You never told me that your mother was fat." I didn't mean it unkindly. I had a fat father. The shock was partly the nineteenth-century awfulness of the word but also that she thought my mother's physical self was something I should have mentioned. The point was that neither of us had described our mother's body to the other. What twelve-year-old girl would? How would we have even brought it up?

That was about the effect that my mother's body had on my childhood. My mother's mother referred to it as a *birth injury* or a *forceps injury*. Not a birth *defect*, a phrase still used in my youth. No human being should be thought of as defective. We got postcards from the March of Dimes featuring smiling children with Kenny sticks, captioned *Help prevent birth defects.*

It was too late to prevent them for the smiling child, so what was the message? All I knew was that my mother didn't approve of the March of Dimes. I assumed they must have been unpleasantly Christian. Or maybe that was Easter Seals.

Mostly in my childhood we used the phrase *She walks with canes.* Accurate, particular. That was what my mother liked in language; she was an editor. She disliked the word *disabled*—"A disabled car doesn't go at all," she pointed out—though she saw nothing wrong with the now-outdated *handicap,* which after all was also used for athletes. I was about to type *elite athletes,* but my mother would hate that, both the canned phrase and the notion that being very good at a game in any way made you elite.

Once, I saw somebody on the internet complain about using the word *lame* to mean stupid or lousy or just not good. I called my mother up.

"Do you mind when people use *lame* to mean bad?" I asked. I probably had some contempt for the notion in my voice. After all, I never thought of my mother when I called something lame. I was certain she'd say no. It was almost impossible to offend her, through her combination of having heard it all and because of her weapons-grade self-confidence and self-definition.

"I hate it," she said plainly. "I think it's awful."

How could I have not known this? How many times had I used it in her presence?

A hatred of professional sports and her idiosyncratic perambulation: two of the many things that made her unusual. Everyone in her family was unusual in one way or another: aunts, uncles, cousins. *Quirky,* somebody once called my mother. What a colossally condescending word: I hate it. It means you've decided that you don't have to take that person seriously.

My mother's body was just her body. I can't tell you what it meant to her. I can say that I don't think it made much of a difference in my childhood. You couldn't run wildly around my mother, for fear of kicking one of her canes out from under her; we parked nearer stores because of our license plate; I went to the beach with other people; we didn't ride escalators; I was never allowed to push the grocery cart; every now and then she fell spectacularly to the ground. In public some people would talk to me instead of her. "Tell her to watch her step," a lady in a department store would say, and I would theatrically trip, and my mother would say, "Watch your step." My mother's body was like my father's stutter. It always surprised me when somebody else noticed and commented.

I don't mean to say that's all my mother's body meant to her parenting, but it was all that I saw. She didn't transcend her body—it was her beloved body—it was just that her personality was more interesting. Impossible to pick out how any of us are shaped by the accidents of our births. I've always hated the notion, in life or in fiction, that the human personality is a puzzle to be solved, that we are a single flashback away from understanding why this person is cruel to her children, why that man on the bus has a dreamy, downcast look. A human being is not a lock, and the past is not a key. *Be kind, because everyone is fighting their own battle.* Yeah, OK, but could they fight it away from me?

When I was a grown person, my mother casually mentioned that her parents had a large iron tank built in their basement so my mother could take water therapy, a detail so strange and beautiful and interesting that I, a vampire, was furious she hadn't mentioned it before: the stories I might have written based on that tank! Perhaps she didn't find it interesting, or perhaps it belonged to an entire category of things she didn't talk about. When I was a child, my mother's childhood felt very close. A happy childhood, she always said. Her parents were respected people in Valley Junction, and wonderful, especially her father, who died before I was born. They were practicing Reform Jews of the melting pot years. My mother insisted that Christmas was a secular holiday. Even my midwestern grandmother, granddaughter of an Orthodox rabbi, grew up with Christmas stockings at the end of her bed and was such a Christmas fanatic we called her Fezziwig. She knitted us Christmas stockings, my mother's gussied up with sequins and satin bows and little metal bells. My mother had a nice boyfriend at Valley High named Frank; in my bedroom was a stuffed dog he had won for her at a carnival, named after him. She had the run of the dime store and the clothing store. She loved her little sister (littler by three minutes) and the extensive train set they had throughout the house. On weekends I watched some of the same movies my mother had loved, on our local UHF station, and listened to the same music. She loved Nat King Cole singing "Nature Boy" and Judy Garland singing "The Trolley Song."

Once, while doing some research in Valley Junction—I had decided to write the great Iowa Jewish novel; that seemed a niche I could fill—I was introduced to a man who'd grown up there. Did he know my grandparents, I asked. He did. I explained that my mother was one of the twins. "Oh, yeah, I remember them," he said. "One of them was retarded, right?"

I reeled. I froze. I gaped. I did any of those things fictional characters do upon hearing an unanswerable question.

There was plenty my mother didn't tell me about being disabled and Jewish in small-town Iowa. Her memory for unhappiness and misery was terrible. Maybe she willed this into being and maybe it was neurological, but somehow I have inherited this tendency—of all my inheritances, it is my favorite, the most useful, though I do remember some grudges. She was (*have I mentioned this?* my mother herself would joke) stubborn. It served her well. She hid a lot of hard work and heartbreak. She wouldn't take no for an answer, but that doesn't mean people didn't say no or you can't or don't or we can't, all the time. I don't know what doctors advised her about having children. At some point she decided she wouldn't be deterred from a single thing she wanted to do, and she did it with good cheer. Not the good cheer of the storybook cripple (as my seventh-grade friend had called her), looking on the bright side, a bird in a cage. My mother's good cheer was an engine that would burn you if you tried to touch it, hoping to switch it off. Her body was her body. It wasn't something to overcome or accept any more than yours was.

My parents were terrible with money. (I'm not much better.) My father's problem was a convoluted laziness. He once rented a car for a year, repeatedly renewing the agreement, because he just couldn't manage to get his own car to the body shop after a crash. (The crash itself was mysterious. The only way in which my father's impressive mind dimmed in old age was geographically and automotively: He got lost; he did peculiar things while driving.) After he died, my mother found, hidden behind books, $24,000 in savings bonds that he had likely just forgotten about. Certainly they should have hired someone to give them advice, but, as with the house, at some point it must have seemed too late and too embarrassing. My mother decided she wouldn't think about money unless she had to. When my father died, we discovered that he had taken out a $200,000 home-equity loan—apparently because that seemed easier than cashing in part of their retirement accounts during their actual retirements—and for years my mother paid only the minimum on it, automatically debited. She set up everything for automatic debit, so that she didn't have to feel the sting of writing checks. Thinking about money made her anxious. She tried not to.

Two months before she died, she called to borrow money—just to get her through the month, she said—and I loaned it. Then she called a week later for another loan. Then the next day. We talked about money and straightening hers out. "How much credit-card debt do you have?" I asked her. "Not much," she said, "not too much. I'll add it all up." *Not much* turned out to be $42,000. We worked on figuring out her financial situation. I pretended to be savvy. On this subject I was patient and helpful: I couldn't've untangled her finances, but I could find somebody whose job that was, and in the meantime I could loan her money so that her monthly automatic payment to the IRS wouldn't bounce. After her death I called her tax accountant, a good man who adored my mother. "She was so *stubborn*," he said to me in a sudden passion. Meaning: She refused to adjust her withholding and always had to pay off what she owed monthly, even when they'd settled the debt my father had incurred through inattention.

After she died it became clear that she was fine, plenty

of money in her various retirement accounts that she should have been spending on her retirement. Somebody had told her long ago—perhaps in childhood—that you should never touch your principal. She passed this advice to me, though we didn't have any principal when I was growing up. I'm not sure I knew what it meant. She could have had such a good time with that money. She hadn't picked up a check in years, but once upon a time that had been one of her great pleasures. She was a stealthy grabber of checks or a show-off, depending on what the occasion and company called for. "This is my party," she liked to say.

She kept the wolves at bay by pretending there were no wolves. Somebody else would throw the party. That was fine, as long as she was invited.

The morning of Halloween 2018, I'd wired her another thousand-dollar loan, and she called me up and said, "You're a good kid. You must have had a *wonderful* mother." That wasn't the last thing she said to me, but it was close.

The day before the estate sale, I let myself into my parents' house. Everything had been minutely rearranged. There were tchotchkes I'd never seen out on tabletops, art in unexpected places on the wall. Nothing had been priced yet: From the time I had handed the key over to the estate-sale guy until after the last customer, he was in charge of every item, had photographed it and advertised it. The agreement I'd signed said the family was allowed to be present for the sale but that some people found it upsetting. I wasn't upset now. The downstairs was in pretty good shape; my mother had paid to clean it. Anything upsetting was above my head.

The house felt wrong, I could tell that, but I could no longer remember what went where, what objects had gone to what relative. This was a better order, I understood. Arranged to draw people in, because now, for the first time, the purpose of the house was to admit strangers. It was a public sale. The public would come.

All those things, now for purchase, what I'd grown up with and what had been in boxes for years. This wasn't a mere estate sale; it wasn't a single estate. It was a fossil record of a family, though incomplete. When my father's parents' Des Moines house was closed up, in the late 1980s, he let movers fill a truck full of furniture and books and bring it to Massachusetts. I remember the day I walked into the house—I'd moved out by then—to see the towers of end tables, one on top of another, each tower with a pleased cat at the top. Eventually some boxes were taken to the basement, and tables drifted into corners where tables made sense. A few years later my mother's mother's apartment was taken apart. My mother's twin sister was in every way her opposite and wanted almost nothing; my mother, being my mother, wanted everything. The house received my grandmother's estate; and before that my grandmother had received a sister's estate; and before that the sister had received another sister's estate: paintings, scrapbooks, the dress shirts of a long-dead husband. Plenty had been dispersed. The considerable remains were for sale.

By the next morning, the estate-sale crew had come through and put on prices. I tried not to absorb what they were. Outside, a line of people waited for the sale to start, a collection of human oddities, by which I mean antique dealers. I could smell the low-voltage excitement and nerves: They'd heard that the lady who'd lived in the house had been here forty years, there were lots of antiques, look at the state of the place, probably a lot of trash inside, maybe something really amazing hidden under the trash. You just had to get in there and lay your hands upon it.

The estate-sale people had set up card tables at the back of the house with the cashbox and some of the more valuable items. That was the checkout.

"You ready?" the main guy said. "We'll start right at nine, let 'em in and out through the laundry room."

"I think so," I said.

"Good crowd," he said. "I think it's gonna be good."

What would my mother have thought? She liked flea markets, but she wasn't much on yard sales. *Too much dross*, she might have said, but, also, she could never be sure of the terrain. Maybe this was why my mother had no interest in cemeteries, or ending up in one, despite a love of the morbid. She collected mourning jewelry, including chains woven out of the hair of the dead; she made dark jokes. Too many steps without banisters in cemeteries, too many stones on the path. When I'd asked her about what she might like to happen after she died, she said, "I plan to die on trash night, so I can be put out in a Hefty bag." Also, she was a cheapskate: She disapproved of spending on the dead what could go to the living.

At nine, the dealers were let inside. Soon enough they came out, arms full. I'd looked at nearly everything in the house before hiring the company and had taken what I wanted—some books, some art, most of my mother's jewelry, which filled two suitcases—and I was surprised by what I felt now. A lady in a black wig and a pink fanny pack set two teapots on the table, and I thought, *But I want those.* A man came out with a pair of Bert and Ernie puppets, and I thought, *Mine.* If something was cheap, I thought, *I might as well have kept that.* If the estate-sale company charged a surprisingly high price and it sold, I thought, *If I'd known it was worth so much, I would have kept it.* But I had my own accumulation, my own dumb things I should get rid of.

What I felt wasn't overwhelming. It was fine. I wasn't watching the dismantling of my parents' house but a peculiar endorsement of their taste. I'd imagined that being here would seem like simply another piece of the work of my mother's death. Cremation, hospital bills, get the lawn mowed, arrange the memorial. Call the old friends. Find a realtor. But the estate sale—it was oddly cheering. It would not only pay for the cleaning out of the house (which would have cost thousands of dollars), but it meant all these weird things, the collections and unlovely heirlooms, would belong to someone else.

"Somebody told me you're the daughter," a woman said to me. She was in her forties, narrow and upright, familiar though I knew we hadn't met. "I just have to say, I was overwhelmed with emotion inside. Somebody was Jewish? Yeah, my mother, too. I just felt when I was in there—these people *loved* this house. I could tell they were interesting, right? I bought a piece of art. I was so drawn to it. A mid-century charcoal of a woman."

"It's probably by my aunt," I said. "My mother's sister. She's an artist."

"We have artists in the family, too. I can't explain it—I just saw this and I was *drawn* to it. Can I show you?"

From her husband she got a pile of papers. Some old maps, an aged issue of *Punch*. Then she extracted a drawing by some excellent artist unknown to me. It was captioned *In the Basement*.

"That's my mother," I said. "I've never seen this drawing before."

Her eyes were cast down. The artist had captured her heavier lower lip, her long nose. The eyebrows. I could feel the woman's eyes on me but also those of the guy in charge of the estate sale, who'd made it clear: Everything in the house was for sale. No takesie backsies. I hadn't even known that this drawing existed. I wished she hadn't shown it to me, that I had been kept ignorant.

"Do you want it back?" she asked.

I had never had it in the first place. "No," I lied.

"Are you sure?"

"1954," I said, looking at the date. "She was in college."

"Do you want it?"

But I have always been bad at answering such questions. I wanted her to give it to me; I felt full of artificial generosity for not snatching it back.

"It's fine," I said.

I wondered how much it had cost her. Probably a dollar or two. She was a very nice woman; she just didn't know me.

My mother, the confounding optimist, always said that her greatest regrets in life were things she didn't buy. Then again, she was better at answering simple questions than I was and at clearly saying what she wanted.

The estate-sale crew—the boss, and a friendly lady with a thick Boston accent, and two or three other young men—stood behind the folding tables with the valuable items: some jewelry; cameras (my father had owned hundreds; these were the priciest); a small archive of papers about the founding of the Boston Symphony Orchestra, which my father must have got at an antique store; a draft of the screenplay of *Misery*, an utter mystery; some foreign money. A painting of a sideshow by a great-aunt. Boxes of old toys.

The drunk neighbor came by. She was a nice woman whom I'd never seen sober, about my age, with doleful blue eyes. She hugged me, as she had the other times we'd met; it was still the age of casual hugs. We stood together in my mother's driveway and she said, "You'll always remember her." Yes, I said. "Love doesn't end with death." No. "Like my son," she said, "he's been dead four-teen years now, and it's like it was yesterday. That kid. He was such a good guy. You know about my son? He fin-ished college and he said, Ma, I'm going to New Zealand. You know: He was young. So he went to New Zealand, and he went everywhere on a motorcycle—wasn't crazy about that, but everywhere he went, he wrote. Pictures, you know, here we are, pictures of the ocean: He surfed. Then he was staying with friends. And one morning he woke up, and I guess he forgot where he was, and he opened the door, and he stepped out, except there wasn't anything out this door, it was a straight drop down, and he just fell. And he was there for hours. And the lady who found him—oh my God," said my mother's drunk neighbor, with the smile of a person speaking about the theoretically unspeakable, who only wants you to listen; I have worn that smile myself. "My God, I feel so sorry for that lady."

The decanters sold, but none of the teacups. The art sold, but none of the furniture. Some books. My parents had never used this back door—no banister, too small. A large unkempt man came through it, clutching some china figurines that I had last seen in Des Moines, Iowa. Big head, square Joan of Arc haircut. He looked like a nerdy ogre. "People!" he said. "You know, I was up there, and some guy turns to me and says, 'This place is a dump,' and I tell him, 'Listen, this is somebody's home.' Respect. *Respect*. You don't know. You don't know the whole story.

Maybe there's not family there. Maybe they don't have kids looking after them. Sure, it's not ideal. But you don't know. There were old people living here. You can tell that. Sad stories everywhere. Could happen to you." He laughed, stepped off the little concrete stage and onto the driveway. "I'm telling you, man. Families."

Even before my mother's disastrous surgery in 2011, my parents were prolific callers of 911. My mother was so stiff that if she fell down, she couldn't get herself up, and my father, also unsteady on his feet, couldn't help her. So they called the EMTs. Far away in Texas, I was only sort of aware of this.

One of the oddities of her long incarceration was that, at the very end, my parents ended up in the same nursing home, in the same room. I can't remember what my father had gone into the hospital for, only that he asked to be discharged to this particularly awful nursing home for the two days of physical therapy they insisted he needed. Perhaps I sound cynical. Despite my conversations with the social workers, my mother was deemed fit for discharge only the day before her annual Medicare nursing-home benefit ran out. My father would be sprung first, and I flew to help get the house in order. I'd already arranged for a long metal ramp to be installed off their wooden front porch—my father hadn't liked the aesthetics of it—and hired cleaners who specialized in crime scenes. My father was so delighted by his freedom that he celebrated by drinking, and so miserable about the cleaning that he treated the misery by drinking, and then, unaccustomed after his hospital stay to drinking, he stopped. By early evening, he called me—I was staying at a friend's nearby—and said, "My chest hurts. Do you think I should call an ambulance?" Yes, I said, I'd be right there.

The EMTs and I arrived at the same time. As they took my father away on a gurney—he was fine, just hungover—one of the EMTs told me, "This house is way cleaner than the last time we were here."

So my father was in the hospital when my mother finally came home. She had ordered herself a hospital bed from Amazon and a diminutive armchair with a lift to set her on her feet, though she still couldn't walk—she'd gone into the hospital not walking, had returned not walking—and she needed human help. She'd hired members of two families of women, Irish and Haitian, and for a while there was somebody there twenty-four hours a day. My father came home. I flew back to Texas. My dear friend Marguerite, herself familiar with domestic chaos, familiar with my parents since she and I were teenagers, stopped by to check in for me. Things were good, she reported. In a voice of wonder, she added, "I think they're better than they have been for years." She meant: The aides kept the house clean, and made sure my parents got out, and opened windows, and kept everything oiled and working. For the first time in years, I didn't have to worry about a catastrophe: my parents dying in a fire, my father dying of a heart attack and leaving my mother, unable to get out of bed, to starve to death. The house no longer felt like a booby trap.

Those strange and bustling women drove my father nuts. He didn't walk much by then, either. He ordered rollators—extra-large rolling walkers, the sort with hand brakes and a fold-down bit you could sit on—and he sat and used his feet to roll through the house backward. He bought a number of reachers, long aluminum arms with a trigger at one end and a pinching mechanism at the other for picking up distant things. In this way my father made himself over into an unambitious robot.

One night when they'd been home—*out of the jug,* as my father put it—for a couple of months, he called me up, his voice sodden with chardonnay but joyous. "I did it!" he said. "I lifted your mother into her bed!"

What? My mother's hospital bed was in the dining room, along the wall where the bookshelves had once been. It wasn't a good hospital bed, but it was good enough, motorized so that it could go up and down, and with a railing so that in the middle of the night my mother could grab hold of it to rearrange her body when she cramped up.

"Where were the aides?" I asked.

"I had to wait till they went out." He was *crowing;* that was the only word for it. "It took a lot of practice, but I did it!"

I tried to picture what had happened. My father in his rollator snugged up next to my mother in her wheelchair. His long arms fitting in around her. She'd wince or she'd bite back the pain, because this was important to him. She was terrible at telling him no. Conditioned not to. Certain mid-century failings, as I said. I didn't think he could have really lifted her. At most, he might have bobbled her to the edge of the bed and rolled her over.

"Maybe soon," said my father, and now his voice wasn't merely proud but full of fury, "maybe finally we can get rid of these goddamn *women*."

The story of my mother's life was not the triumph over the body but the triumph *of* the body. My father's was not. My mother said that in the 1950s my father was the tallest person in any crowd; she could look across any room and find him. In those days he was thin or mildly portly. My mother commented on his long arms, how he could reach out and snag something off a table seemingly across the room. She knew the measure of all limbs. Her own arms were short, and she cursed them. She had, she said often, her father's arms; he had his shirts tailored especially for his stumpy appendages. Did my mother know these things about her own body because she lived in it or because she was the daughter of a clothing-shop owner? Her shoulders were so narrow, shoulder bags slid from them, and she owned special hooked brooches that pinned on like epaulets to catch straps. She was short-waisted, small-busted, particularly compared to her bosomy mother. She was short, though not always: She and her twin sister had been, she assured me, the tallest kids in school till the fourth grade, and then they just stopped. Four foot eleven and three-quarter inches, she told me. For a long time I believed if she stood as straight as possible—if she steadied herself on a wall and assumed her full height—she would be that tall, a tiny bit taller than me. But I don't think that's true.

My mother had always found a way to *go*. She got her driver's license as a teenager and drove our various terrible family cars, one foot on the gas and one on the brake, which was theoretically illegal but all her stiff legs were capable of. The first car I remember is our Renault, brought back from Paris on a boat, which eventually wouldn't reverse; my parents kept driving it anyhow. We had a Volvo that had to be turned on with a screwdriver. An enormous early-1970s (it was the mid-1980s) green Cadillac with a bench seat, perhaps the very reason I didn't learn to drive till years later, because my long-legged father couldn't sit in the front seat with me, and my short-legged mother couldn't see over the dashboard to give me useful advice. Finally, the navy-blue Caddy with the broken driver's seat, which my father fixed with a case of empty beer bottles at a convenient distance from the pedals for him. My mother would have needed two cases of beer. That's when she stopped driving at all.

My father didn't take care of his body any better than he took care of cars. He liked both cream sauces and deep-fried food. He liked both red wine and Drambuie. Sometimes he smoked: menthols, cloves, cigars. After his first heart attack, in his fifties, he reformed for a while, put a treadmill in the basement and changed his diet and drank only red wine. I'm not sure when the reformation ended. One of the reasons he hated having the aides around: their disapproval of his various cherished bad habits—eating what he wanted; drinking wine when he wanted; snapping at my mother for small irritations as he had for decades. Worse, the aides were sympathetic to my mother but less so to him, as everyone was. *You made your body, now you have to lie in it.*

"Don't lift her," I said to him on the phone, even though I knew it would make him angry. He wasn't asking my permission; he only wanted to share his happiness. "It's not safe."

But he and my mother knew: When you're old, safety is overrated. Safety is the bossy Irish lady, who is, after all, your employee, taking away your wineglass, saying, "That's enough, that's enough now, that's enough now, darlin'." Safety puts you in a nursing home and turns you over regularly so that you do not die in your sleep.

You could be kept for years if you weren't careful, like a roped-off chair in a museum that nobody is allowed to sit in, which makes it only something shaped like a chair. Watch out for safety. It will make you no longer yourself, only an object shaped that way.

After my father's memorial service I took my mother to New York, drove her back to Boston, and slept on the sofa for the few hours before my early-morning flight. At 2:00 A.M., I heard my mother calling for me: She'd got herself out of bed to go to the bathroom, but she'd forgotten to ask me to take off her socks and had slid to the ground, unhurt. One of her talents. I tried to lift her, but she was so stiff, and I so weak, I could get her only inches off the ground. "Call 911," she said. "I can't call 911 just to lift you," I said, exhausted, semi-conscious. It felt immoral to me, or illegal. I tried to lift her over and over. "Hand me the phone and I'll call," said my mother, and she did, and they got her up, made her sign a piece of paper that said she refused to be taken to the hospital, and left. Routine, for everyone but me. My biceps were sore for a week afterward.

On the evening of Halloween 2018, my mother called to say that she'd fallen and the paramedics had come and put her in her recliner and she was absolutely fine. "Are you sure?" I asked. "Yes," she said, though she sounded uncharacteristically shaken. I can't remember everything we said, but she was concerned, as she often was, about her walking. "I'm especially stiff," she said. "Who do you think we can get to help me with my perambulation?" I suggested some people we could ask.

"I'll talk to you tomorrow," I said.

She said, "Goody." Then she said, "So what's the agenda?"

"What agenda?"

She repeated, "Who can we get to help me with my perambulation?"

"I'm sure we'll think of somebody," I said. I remembered the kind, puppyish doctor who'd said to me years before, *At this age, nearly everything manifests as confusion.* She was shaken up. She'd just been seen by medical professionals. I would talk to her first thing tomorrow.

But the next person I talked to was somebody who called at three in the morning from the hospital, to say that my mother had been admitted. She was unconscious. They hadn't yet figured out why.

I still don't know who summoned the EMTs a second time.

In London, I'd planned to wander the whole day, from museum to museum, pub to restaurant, but the fabric of my wandering started to unravel, from tiredness or sorrow. My knee hurt. There were too many people. I wasn't lonely, I told myself severely. I knew people who lived in London, but their numbers weren't in my cheap phone. Once upon a time I might have found an internet café, back in the days when the cities of the world were full of such things, before we all became self-sufficient. I thought about dialing my childhood phone number, my mother's phone number, though nobody would have answered. The house was empty; the phones had been unplugged; the phone number existed only because the internet did, and the internet existed because I hadn't managed to unplug it yet. There were so many things that naturally ended when a person died, and so many things you had to put a stop to.

Ahead of me, Big Ben was hidden in a sleeve of scaffolding—no, not Big Ben, as my father would have pointed out; Big Ben was the bell, not the clock, not the clock tower. The day was warm but tolerable. I went more slowly than I would have if my mother were still alive and heading down the sidewalk on her scooter. She was always in a hurry, especially in cities, headed to a museum or a theater. Sometimes she would hit the throttle so hard I had to run to keep up with her, or I'd lose her in the crowd.

There were three productions of *A Midsummer Night's Dream* in London that summer. The best-reviewed was near Tower Bridge on the South Bank. There might still be tickets. My mother would have called it *Midsummer*; I liked to tease her about her abridgements of play titles. *Streetcar, Salesman*—the casual inside references of the True Theater Person. My father was a minor theater person, a scholar, one foot firmly in the text, and he disapproved of setting Shakespeare anywhere but in the time specified by Shakespeare himself, disapproved of any costumes that didn't exist in Shakespeare's time or before. *I am a purist; you are unimaginative; he is an old stick-in-the-mud.* In my childhood we went to a lot of plays as a family. My father would drop us off at the entrance before parking the car; we would go in, settle into our seats. Somehow my father always managed to arrive just as the lights dimmed, and you could hear the palpable, complicated outrage of the person in the seat behind him, realizing their good luck—a clear view of the stage—had turned to the worst possible luck, a total eclipse. Also, my father tended to fall asleep and snore.

By the time I was a teenager, I was my mother's usual theater date, being open-minded if still judgmental. I was an audience member: I might dislike a production, but I never thought of how I would have done things differently. My mother recast in her mind, re-costumed, re-blocked. As far as I know, once she gave up the theater—sometime before I was born, or before I was sentient—she never dabbled, except to think about it. It wasn't in her nature to be an amateur at anything. As a young woman in New York, she got standing-room-only tickets, stood to see *Under Milk Wood* and *Auntie Mame*. I try to picture her: short, unsteady but upright, before the major surgery of her adulthood, which happened when I was four or so and from which, I think, she never really recovered. I can't see her. There are old films of her and her sister as small children in their backyard but no footage of my mother walking: You would have to notice her serious shoes, unlike her twin sister's patent Mary Janes; her place in the little red wagon (filmed in black-and-white but manifestly red; I remember my mother's stories); her chair with more support and arms for her to hold on to. Once, she came to visit having given up coffee—"You, give up coffee?" I said in a shocked voice. "I don't think

I understand who you are without coffee"—and was so sleepy I had to put her in a similar chair because she kept nodding off and threatening to tumble to the floor. She could fall asleep anywhere. Her greatest feat was dozing off in the Museum of Modern Art with her hand on the throttle of her scooter. She nearly rolled through an installation that involved a pile of sand on the floor. My job at the theater was to nudge her awake, though I inherited the family somnolence and we often napped in tandem.

The last play I saw with my mother, ever, was in London, at an older theater. We'd discovered on one of our trips to New York that if you go to the theater in a scooter or a wheelchair, there are often tickets available at the last minute for you and your companion. *Companion* is the official term. The locations vary in quality—sometimes excellently up close, sometimes at the very back of the house. At this last theater of our lives together, we entered at ground level; instead of going up, the house went down, the stage many feet below street level. This sounds like a dream as I describe it now, or a made-up place. It's *not* a made-up place, though this is a novel, and the theater might be fictional, and my insistence fictional, and my mother the only real thing, though this version of her is also fictional. In this theater the spot for my mother's scooter was a little platform to drive out on. It was much higher than my seat next to her—not satisfactory—so I couldn't nudge her or even see her, and by and by as the actors spoke, their voices got garbled and they said things that confused me and I had fallen asleep and was already being woken by an usher saying, as though he'd found me tucked under the covers in a character's bed on the stage itself, "You can't sleep here!"

It isn't impossible that I was snoring.

My mother loved that story, me even sleepier than her.

Yes, I thought. A play. That's where I would head. I thought about hailing a cab. My mother and I had taken dozens of them on our London trip. They seemed to us like enchanted creatures from a children's book, trained and kindly hippos, land-borne whales. We could stand on the sidewalk and wave and one would come nosing up, having never met us before, and open its doors and take us in, deliver us wherever we wanted (the drivers had the map of London memorized). That was one of the reasons we'd chosen London. Every black cab, every single one, was outfitted with a ramp and therefore was accessible. In Boston she had to arrange transportation the night before at the latest and hope there was room for her. It had been years since my mother had been in a city and gone wherever she wanted, no advance notice, very little struggle. When we went to New York I rented a car, which meant helping her off the scooter and into the passenger's seat, disassembling the scooter—more than once I lightly damaged it—and putting it in the trunk. Then the reverse at the next place. That fold-down London-black-cab ramp: a piece of genius. The law that mandated it: civilized. My mother drove right in. If she had lived in London and had money enough, she could have gone anywhere she liked. She could go somewhere on the spur of the moment; she could go somewhere without anyone she knew being aware of it. It's not poignant, knowing that at home she couldn't. It's enraging.

When I moved to Texas in my early forties, I told myself that it wasn't so far from Boston, just three and a half hours on a direct flight, or the same amount of time as the Boston–to–New York train. Anybody could look at a map and see what a dolt I was. There weren't direct flights all day long. I could not, if my parents needed me, jump in a car and drive from Texas to Boston, not in a handful of hours, not even if I drove all day and night. Sometimes my mother ended up in the hospital and would call me and tell me, "In the name of full disclosure . . ." When I offered to come, she would say, "Not now. Come in a month, when we can have fun." In this way I missed the installation of her pacemaker. I'd moved far away, as far away as London is from St. Petersburg, and it felt it.

Just past the Houses of Parliament, a man and woman stood on the corner, holding up enormous red signs that said, WE VOTED TO LEAVE. I was certain they were married. WE VOTED TO LEAVE—a modest claim, really, in its utter vagueness and the unclarity of the antecedent. The antecedent for *we* was properly *the United Kingdom*, but looking at them you could sense the weariness in their arms, and it seemed as though *we* meant only *them*, Mr. and Mrs. Redshirt, possibly of Tunbridge Wells. It wasn't my country, so though I thought they were jerks, I didn't hate them, as I would have if I had seen somebody holding a sign with that awful imperative MAKE AMERICA GREAT AGAIN. I mean, I wouldn't have voted to leave. But historically and under other circumstances, I had.

"I want a black cab," my mother said, every single time we were nestled in the back of one, which was often, the pleasure in deciding to cross London on a whim was so great. "Just one black cab."

I said, "I wish I could buy you one."

I kept walking.

I kept walking. It's not much of a plot. As a fictional character I do very little of consequence, even though as a writer my favorite thing about fiction is its ability to anatomize consequence. Emotional and active consequence, which is how I think about plot: Plot is what occurs and what the characters feel, with real plot the attraction and repulsion between event and emotion.

Why I don't like writers as characters in fiction: The action feels false. Any action would. Fictional writers go on trips, instead of droning on about the work of writing and how *hard* it is and how you have to write *every* day and the misery of it all and here's how to think about structure and how nobody would voluntarily choose this work if they were good at anything else (this is an actual thing I once heard a successful writer tell an audience of aspiring writers at a conference) and here is a tip for making your dialogue sharper. In the real world, if you cut a novelist, you'll get a craft talk or a complaint. As for me, I don't think writing is that hard, as long as you're comfortable with failure on every single level.

I don't believe in craft. At least, I don't think about craft when I write. I might not think at all when I write. Might not do anything on purpose. "Must be nice not to have to work for a living," my mother would say to me in those rare periods I supported myself only with writing.

In writing, *I am not good at* often means *I am not interested in,* and vice versa. I used to not believe in plot because I wasn't interested: All my plots were about time. That might have been because not much had happened to me, not so much as a broken bone. Then a few things did befall me, and I understood plot in a different way: I discovered that a single event could alter the course of a life. My short stories, especially, were different after that. Not necessarily better, but I and they were changed.

You think you're one sort of writer. For years, you believe it. You have to: Otherwise, you'd never get any work done.

Nothing wrong with time as plot: A character is born and is on their way to death and here's everything between. I wish I could write a book like this about my mother, David Copperfield except Jewish, and disabled, and female, and an American wiseacre, but there's too much I don't know and I can't bear to make up.

Even now I can only tell you what plot isn't. It's not a mysterious animating spirit that lives at the center of fiction, without which a novel or story dies. It isn't a motor, a mechanical thing, also at the center of the work, also without which the work is dead. It's as idiosyncratic as anything in fiction: language, character. It belongs to you.

"I'm going to start to say something," I tell my students, "and we'll see if I still believe it by the end of the sentence." I usually do. I'm very credulous when it comes to my own writing advice: I'm a sucker for a turn of phrase with the ring of truth. Later, my belief evaporates.

I could teach almost anyone how to write a certain kind of fiction, what's sometimes called "a workshop story," written mostly in scene, in first or third person, attached to a single point of view, lightly populated, nothing out of the ordinary, mostly inside a house, probably in a kitchen, in which the exact location and temperature of every beverage is known—the beer warm, the coffee cold. You could write this story, and nothing would be wrong with it. Not a thing untoward. Not a thing out of place. But would you recognize it in your dreams?

I am only one person, I sometimes tell my students. What I mean is, don't take my word for it, listen to other people; other writers believe different things (though I'm my mother's daughter and generally believe that I'm right). I am only one person, I tell myself when I worry that my work isn't relevant, doesn't speak to our moment, isn't timeless, doesn't contain the world and all its worries. I am only one person, I tell myself when I disagree with the world, or when I read about *the writing community,* since I became a writer for the solitary nature of the work: I like writers one at a time well enough and a couple dozen I even love, and one I love particularly, but when they gather, I cannot bear their company. I wish them all well. They are not my community. I am only one person. Any woman writer with children will be asked about motherhood and writing, and it's a good question for some people, but for me, as a writer, I am only one person. Boldly, wearily, cheerfully: I insist on my singularity. When I write about my mother and my family and worry whether I have the right, I assure myself, I am only one person. Every one person is allowed their own story.

Some members of a family might never really trust the writer in their midst. With good reason? You tell me.

By which I mean: The fictional me is unmarried, an only child, childless. The actual me is not. (The fictional me is the narrator of this book. The actual me is the author. All Cretans are liars; I myself am a Cretan.) No, I'm telling the truth now, I swear. I have a brother, and some offspring, and am married. I love everyone and I want to keep them safe, safe from me particularly. Long ago—by which I mean before I had children—I had firm feelings about the relationship between children and their parents' literary works. I would read memoirs and primly think, *But what will your children think when they read that?* Back then I thought the duty of a parent was to remain a mysterious monolith of love and care. I no longer do. It's impossible, one way or the other. But I have left my living family out.

(How is it being married to another writer, I am sometimes asked, and the answer is: I would hate being married to another writer; it's a dreadful proposition, except the particular writer I married. Dear young writers in love with other writers: Only stay with somebody whose work you love and understand and want to live with for the rest of your life, for whom the feeling is mutual. I'm only dispensing advice about writing; I have no advice about love. All my advice is about love.)

When people said to me, "You should write about your parents," I always said, "Not when they're alive," not because they were awful—they were wonderful—but because they were odd and extraordinarily private and I didn't feel I could write about them with any kind of honesty—a necessity, even in, especially in, fiction—if I knew they were going to read it. Sometimes I wonder what I might have written about my parents earlier, when they were younger and alive and I was young myself. What I might have understood more deeply because I had translated it into words, the only way I have understood anything in my life. The things I might have been mad at or was unbothered by then and only got mad at later. What I've forgotten, moments of love, bitterness, turns of phrase used only once. Facts; confessions. *You could have written it all down just for yourself,* a nonwriter might say. Impossible. No, I had to wait. But I regret it, too.

Why impossible? Because for a writer the proper end of a book is publication. I have written several books that haven't been published. Not my aim: Two of them I wrote without enough forethought, with characters whose souls were goldfish, harmless, picturesque. Two my editor at the time turned down after years of work, which were like ships going down. For some years I felt ashamed at the failure of these novels and didn't talk about them. Now I don't, and I do. But those books trouble me. An unpublished book is an ungrounded wire.

No book I've published troubles me. I don't claim this is a sign of good character. I'm an appalling show-off, lifelong, a form of self-protection: I am an animal that puffs up and changes color so you'll notice that instead of my true form. I learned this from my mother, the extrovert, who knew that people will gawk and all you can hope is to misdirect them.

There are no agreed-upon safety precautions for writing. Unlike some pursuits, if you hurt yourself, it's a sign that you're doing it right. Beginners are much more likely to emerge from the process unscathed, because they're not inclined to scathe themselves. Few of us are naturals at it.

Why do I write? To try to get human beings on a page

without the use of vivisection or preservatives or a spiritualist's props, to make them seem lively still.

As a writer, I claim to be modest, but I have delusions of grandeur. I call them delusions in order to sound modest.

The man at the Bridge Theatre box office looked like the explosives expert in a heist movie. He wore a sweater vest; he had a soft mustache. I couldn't place him on the scale between irony and geekery, for I grew up in the days of unironic mustaches.

"Any tickets for tonight?" I asked.

"Just the one?"

"Alas."

His mustache twitched. I didn't know the impetus of the twitch—sympathy, amusement, English embarrassment at what might have seemed a lament about my own singularity. He showed me the theater's seating plan, which wasn't in the round but in the square, rows of seats at right angles on four sides.

"The standing tickets are in the pit," he said. He gave me a serious look; this was serious information. "You'll be amidst the action. Part of the performance."

There are no words more terrifying than *audience participation*. If I run for president, it will be with the slogan *Rebuild that fourth wall!*

"Sounds awful," I said.

"Some people like it," he said, in a pleasant school-teacher's voice, by which I mean, I was being graded and I was failing.

"I'm sure—it's not for me."

With the eraser end of a pencil, he indicated the places I could sit. I'd been to plays in England often enough that I knew the close-in seats were called the Stalls and the upper balcony was called the Gods. Perhaps that was meaningless in a small, new theater like this. I picked a high-up seat, just in case the audience participation splashed out of the pit and into the front row.

I joined the crowd in the lobby. My fellow theatergoers! Though I often tell myself that I dislike people—those receptacles for opinions and philosophies and behaviors that are not my own—I love being a member of an audience. We're all doing the same thing, we didn't prearrange it but here we are, and the performance will be different because it's *us*, exactly *us*, in the seats. We stand shoulder to shoulder in the lobby beforehand, buying our drinks, ordering snacks for the intermission—the *interval*, as it's called in England. I miss the interval, rushing to the restroom, the concession stand; I miss walking out into the air after the last act, detaching myself from my fellow audience members, going home by myself.

I got a glass of prosecco, ordered another ahead of time for the interval, went in and found my spot on the bench seat. The house was tiered like a wedding cake, at an extreme rake: Even my father wouldn't've blocked the view of the person behind him. I leaned on the rail in front of me and slipped off my shoes and cooled my feet on the floor. I missed my mother. I mean, I kept missing her, but in a theater the missing took on a bodily quality. She should be at my left elbow, with her own glass of prosecco, wearing her cheap reading glasses, looking at the program. Still, a play on my own was delightful. The pit was filled with brave and thrifty fools who were willing to be part of the performance. I waited for the lights to go down.

In the spring of my first year of graduate school, my grandmother brought one of her younger sisters from Florida to live in Des Moines. It was a relocation of force: My great-aunt had lived in New York for years, was a nonconformist, notably eccentric even among their nine other unconventional siblings, had painted the clowns of the Ringling Bros. and Barnum & Bailey circus, and when she got to a certain age did not run away with the circus but attempted to retire with it, had moved near the circus's winter home in Sarasota, Florida, where she was unhappy and confused. I went to Des Moines to help unpack boxes, but it was clear: My aunt had Alzheimer's, which had killed two other sisters, hard in this case to notice because she had been strange and impulsive all her life. Even in Des Moines my grandmother refused to say *Alzheimer's* aloud, though she must have suspected that was the problem. Wanted to protect her sister's privacy, even as my aunt attended social events at the temple and rummaged through other people's purses, agitated that she couldn't find the keys to her Florida house. She had a temper. She yelled at us. I tried to let her yell at me more than at my grandmother, because I could take it: She had never known who I was.

All spring I was back and forth on the Greyhound bus from Iowa City. I couldn't conceive of writing fiction, because my head was filled with the emergency that was my aunt's existence, but I had a deadline for workshop, so I wrote about my time with my grandmother and aunt and called it "a nonfiction short story." The reception, as I recall, was particularly terrible. "What does this even mean?" one of my classmates asked. "A nonfiction short story. Which is it, fiction or nonfiction? *It matters.*"

He wasn't asking me—I wasn't allowed to answer—but the other people in the room agreed that I had done something wrong, something authorially intrusive. Authorial intrusion was seen as a great aesthetic crime in the 1980s. We accused one another of it all the time, those moments our shadows fell across our fiction. I can't remember why we thought it was so awful. Maybe it was supposed to be a sign of ego. Imagine: a writer with a visible ego.

The workshop teacher cleared his throat. He was a writer of fiction, but his first book had been a celebrated memoir, and he said, "If I know one thing, it's that it doesn't make any difference. Call it what you want."

I felt physically grateful, as though I had been given an antidote. All these years and pages later, I still can't decide whether I agree with him.

I never showed my grandmother what I'd written about her and her sister, but I dedicated my first book to her and she introduced me at her temple as the youngest person ever to publish a novel, though nothing in that sentence was accurate except that I was a person: The book was not yet out, only sold; it was a collection of short stories; and many younger people had beat me to it.

When my grandmother died of a heart attack in her apartment a few years later, getting dressed for the day, my aunt was living in the Iowa Jewish Senior Life Center, formerly the Iowa Jewish Home for the Aged. My grandmother's memory was still in order; only her nerves were frayed. The woman who cleaned for her found her in the early afternoon, lying across the threshold of her bathroom. "If she could have done anything different," my mother told friends who asked about her mother's death, "she would have finished pulling up her slacks." I finally told my mother to knock it off: If she thought my grandmother would have rather not been found with her slacks down, then she would surely have rather people didn't *know* she'd been found with her slacks down. We flew out for the funeral immediately. She would be buried within three days in the Jewish cemetery, next to her husband, dead then thirty years. We held a reception afterward in the community room of my grandmother's apartment building, where two months before we'd thrown her a party. She'd admitted then that the year's birthday was significant, but she'd never say how old she was. Even her driver's license was wrong.

After the reception, my mother and I went down the hallway into the lobby. We were headed to the elevators, to my grandmother's apartment on the third floor. It's been years now since I've seen it—the way my mother walked with canes, deliberately, with a kind of hitching grace, picking up one cane and setting it down, then the other; I can see it, though I can't describe or explain it, in the way that before Muybridge nobody knew exactly how horses ran. Once, I saw a young woman, decades younger than me, walking through a Target in the exact same hitching way, and tears sprang—sprang, as though from a spring—to my eyes, and I wanted to follow her until I realized what a fucking creep I was.

In my grandmother's lobby, a little old lady sat on the colossal tufted four-sided sofa, facing us. I don't know if it was the same old lady who was always sitting in the lobby or whether she was occasionally replaced, like an ornamental plant.

She called out to my mother, "What happened to you, sweetheart?"

People asked this all the time. To them, my mother's

body itself asked the question, and it was her duty to answer it. Polio? Car accident? She had made them *notice* her, and now she had to explain why.

Without looking at the old woman, my mother said, "Cerebral palsy," and headed to the elevator.

My mother was then fifty-eight years old. I was twenty-six. I had never heard her say the words *cerebral palsy*, not to describe herself, and for a moment they struck me as a solution to something I hadn't known was a puzzle. She'd never used those words before, I understood, because my grandmother hadn't liked them, even though the words my grandmother used—*birth injury*—meant the same thing. The injury, if there had been one, was the event. Cerebral palsy was the result. But my mother hadn't used the words even miles away from my grandmother's hearing. Now my grandmother was dead and my mother could describe herself any way she liked.

I can guess why my grandmother didn't like the phrase. If there was an injury, then there was an injurer, a person—the doctor—who was at fault, someone other than my grandmother herself. My grandmother was thirty-two when my mother and her sister were born, old to become a mother back in 1935. Even my grandmother cannot outrun birth records on the internet. Old enough to have increased her chances of twins. Old enough that the birth could have been tricky. My mother had a birth injury or pre-birth injury; my aunt had congenital heart problems; it could only be (my grandmother might have thought; even when I knew and loved her she was full of self-recrimination) my grandmother's fault.

Or else she didn't like anything with the air of a diagnosis, anything that might reduce her multitudinous darling to a medical term.

After that my mother was never shy with the words.

If this were a memoir—it isn't—the author might talk at length about her own connection to her grandmother on the subject of self-recrimination, how easy it is to blame yourself for the harm that comes to children during pregnancy, and how other people, even well-meaning ones, will blame you, too. It isn't; she won't. No book can contain everything.

The cast of *A Midsummer Night's Dream* was excellent, diverse, beautiful, sultry. The fairyfolk were suspended from the ceiling by silks and trapezes—they swung and wound themselves up and hung upside down. On the ground the set was made of a series of beds at all different levels, with brass headboards and rumpled sheets. The actors jumped from one to another or were wheeled around by stagehands while other stagehands managed the audience in the pit, shepherding them out of the way. I wondered, as ever, whether I'd picked the right seat, whether the play would look different, or better, across the house or on either side.

The actress who played Titania and Hippolyta was famous for a television show I had never seen. She was very blond and pale, beautiful in an odd way, and in Titania's emerald-green gown looked sculpted of vanilla ice cream. The director had decided—oh, my father would have hated it! Just act the text as it was written!—to make a switch. Instead of Oberon bewitching Titania so that she falls in love with the lowly Bottom, Titania does the bewitching, making Oberon the besotted. Another decision, one that moved me peculiarly, interested in scale as I was raised to be: The actors who played the lovers, Hermia and Helena and Demetrius and Lysander, were all quite small, and Titania, Oberon, and Bottom were all well over six feet tall. When it was said of Hermia, "Though she is but little, she is fierce," it seemed to be about human beings in general. Oberon and Bottom in bed together, wheeled around, was one of the sexiest things I've ever seen.

I loved everything about the performance. Would my mother have? Maybe. We didn't always agree about the theater. I took her to see *Fun Home* in New York, and when I asked her at the end whether she liked it, she made a face and gestured *so-so,* and I said passionately, "Well, I *loved* it." She preferred her musicals to have originated as musicals; she reflexively disliked adaptations. I couldn't remember what she'd thought of the three productions we'd seen together in London. Liked them, I think.

When Titania sent off Puck, she did it from bed. Puck was played by a wiry acrobat with a Scottish accent. He scowled through much of the play.

"By some illusion see thou bring him here," the recumbent Titania told him. "I'll charm his eyes against he do appear."

Puck stood on another, higher bed, facing me. "I go, I go. Look how I go," he said, scowling, churlish, his feet apart. "Swifter than arrow from the Tartar's bow."

Then he jumped in the air and made his body a jack-knife and disappeared, toes first, into a slit in the bed none of us had noticed. He fell right through. Through bedclothes, through mattress. He was gone.

We gasped. I am speaking for all of us, the audience. We couldn't believe it. He was as gone as anyone is ever gone, and all of us, onstage, in the pit, in the Gods, in the Stalls, we leaned forward, we wanted—it's amazing that we didn't—to leave our seats and dive down through the mattress to find him. Like Orpheus and Eurydice. Like Mr. Salt and Veruca. We loved him. We couldn't bear to lose him.

My mother's last illness was a brain aneurysm. Either she'd had one, and that caused the fall, or she'd fallen and had hit her head. The doctors thought it was probably the former, but it didn't matter. The effect was the same. Did it matter to me? I supposed I'd prefer an act of God to an act of gravity. I'd always promised my mother that the only way I'd ever allow her to go into a nursing home again would be if she was so far gone she wouldn't notice. After she died, I thought, why did I include a single caveat? But I think my mother would have heard the lie, and I hope she heard the truth.

My brother—my brother whom I adore—went to Boston first, and then I came to replace him. I sat by the hospital bed. I called friends and family, but I didn't do a great job of describing what was going on: I said, *She's not herself,* and one of her closest friends showed up with a plate of cookies that his wife had made—my mother had a sweet tooth; a treat tooth; she loved treats of any kind; she appreciated, as I say, *everything.* My mother was beyond cookies. She was out cold, fed by a nasogastric tube. The doctors explained that if the unconsciousness persisted, they'd have to surgically implant a feeding tube directly into her stomach. I still remember the fondness and grief on the friend's face, looking at my mother unconscious in bed, understanding the seriousness of what had happened. I reassured him.

What did I say to my mother? To the sleeping you might say anything, the way you can to a baby, or a photograph, any silly thing that comes into your head, the way you can declare love to a cat. Nothing in the world changes when you tell a cat, *I love you.* (Once, over the phone, on his birthday, I told my father I loved him; he replied, "Ditto.") In the hospital I did tell my mother that I loved her, but only at the end of the day. I couldn't see her thoughts, not the scantest glimmer of light on the wavelets of her brain, but that was all right. I was awaiting another resurrection.

I'd seen her sleeping face so many times before. It was easy to imagine that she might wake at any time. Not all the way: The sleep was too deep for that; the sleep was a well. But I could imagine her opening her sleepy eyes. If her eyes were open, I could imagine her looking at me. If she looked at me, I could imagine her recognizing me. If she recognized me, I could imagine her smiling ruefully, full of rue, full of rue with a garnish of reproach. If she could smile ruefully and reproachfully, I could imagine her saying something, *Let's get out of here,* or *Let's blow this pop stand,* or *Damnation,* her favorite swear. If she could swear—

In this way, step by step, I could imagine her recovery. Then one day the nurse and the social worker came in to assess her. *Assessment* meant *aggravation:* yelling her name and gently shaking her. They cranked up her bed so she had no choice but to sit. My wonderful second cousin was with me, and two of the women whom my mother employed and loved, who loved her, including her favorite aide, to whom she was very close, who was staying in the house and taking care of the cats. I wouldn't stay in the house unless I had to, had not spent more than a night in literal decades. I always stayed with friends.

My mother slipped down in the bed, because she was stiff. "I'm a stiff old lady," she'd say most days, and toward the end of her life she would report daily on her stiffness. She would say, alarmed, "I'm inexplicably stiff." Alarm because stiffness meant she couldn't walk. *It's not inexplicable,* I thought but never told her. Then the stiffness would wane and she was no longer ossified, just slow and arthritic. That's why she'd asked me, during our last phone call, about finding someone to help her with her perambulation. She was stiff. You had to battle stiffness.

The nurse and social worker pulled her up in the bed and shouted her name and she opened her eyes.

We all of us—the women who worked for her, my cousin, and me, the daughter, *are you the daughter*, all the doctors would say—we rushed forward like minor players in a religious painting having been shown proof. Of what? We didn't know. Her eyes were their ordinary brown. They weren't focused; they looked small in their sockets. We all called her name. This was the first sign of real hope that we had. We had hoped and had been hoping, but only because we still could. Now there were her eyes, and at any moment they would focus on one of us calling her name, a name she'd always been very fond of. She sent presents to any child with the same name. I'd given her a small mid-century bicycle license plate with her name, the sort you might wire to the hoop of a banana seat, and she'd put it on the basket of her scooter, which meant passing strangers saw it and said, *Hello, Natalie! Watch out, here comes Natalie! Hiya, Natalie!*[1]

Was she smiling a little? I think she was.

And I thought, *This is the moment that changes everything.* Which is true: It was that moment exactly. Or it should have been. It should have been the moment that told me she was no longer there. She was gone. As if in a religious painting we rushed forward, but the news of the day was, *No.* The news of the day was, *Not this time.*

---

1   Natalie Jacobson McCracken, 1935–2018

Her eyes opening had been a reflex, not an answer, and it's an awful joke of the body that the two look so much the same.

We took it as a sign of something else, and we lived in hope for several days more.

It's this look that startles into my head at the oddest of times.

The doctors at that hospital liked to say, "How do *you* think your mother's doing?" I presumed this was some sort of empathy training, because they all said it. At first I said, "I'm not sure," but soon enough, in honor of my mother, I would say, "Actually it's very hard to tell, because you see, Doctor, I have zero medical training." The nurse asked me if I wanted to talk to the palliative-care doctor. Sure, I said, thinking one should be prepared for all possibilities. The palliative-care doctor asked me how I thought my mother was doing. When it became clear that I didn't know that she would never recover, that in saying, *Sure, I'd like to talk to the palliative-care doctor*, I was choosing a fork in the road, he became intensely uncomfortable. He was not the doctor who told you that your loved one was going to die; he was the doctor you talked to after you'd been told. But here was a knucklehead lady who'd somehow not gotten the message. He couldn't look me in the eye.

He was a young man, with a slapstick comedian's balletic rubbery gestures. "Let's look at some brain scans," he suggested. So we did.

"See here, where it's white," he said.

She wouldn't like me peering into her brain, I thought, that exceptional and highly exercised organ with which she did everything she loved. The organ that had shaped her body and her entire personality. If I had to look at it, I wished that, like Mrs. Darling, I could tidy it up, move away the dark thoughts, see my mother's Neverland— because in *Peter Pan*, each child has their own Neverland, idiosyncratic, though there is, Barrie tells us, *a family resemblance.*

Of course, it wasn't really my mother's mind I peered into, only a picture of it, taken in an unflattering light from an unflattering angle.

And so I came to understand that this time, my mother would *not* open her eyes and say to me, over and over, *Let's go home. Let's get out of here.* The book I'd brought to read to her this time was Dylan Thomas's *Portrait of the Artist as a Young Dog.* Maybe that had been insufficiently sentimental, though she loved Dylan Thomas in a deep and personal way, had not only seen *Under Milk Wood* on Broadway but directed a production in Madison, Wisconsin.

I called my brother. Soon enough we were talking to people from hospice, and speaking of the feeding tube as artificial nutrition, and unnecessary surgery, and my mother came home for the last time.

My mother's favorite restaurant, she always said, was a place she'd never been before. She liked to eat outside, particularly if she could look at the sea. She liked views of all kinds and commenting on them. The only foods she couldn't bear were peanuts and peanut butter, and it drove her crazy when people suggested she was allergic: She just didn't like the taste. Anything else she ate with gusto—though now I remember she was once presented with a piece of toast spread with Marmite, and she ate it all, and when asked how she liked it, she said, "I'm not eager to repeat the experience." One memorable day on one of my parents' trips to Maine, she consumed five lobsters: twin lobsters at lunch, triplet lobsters at dinner. In their later years my parents often had one late-afternoon meal, which my mother called lupper. She was the most obsessive checker of emails I ever met and a haggler in antique stores. She liked to sing but couldn't carry a tune; a college friend of hers told her he thought she could when she'd had a few drinks and once stayed sober at a party to listen to her, to confirm this. She never learned to play a musical instrument and as an artist could draw slices of watermelon and the backs of bunnies and that was it. Her handwriting was like nobody else's, slanted and angular, odd and legible. She could touch-type at great speed without looking at the keyboard. She loved goats, and the feeling appeared to be mutual: In the petting zoos of my youth, when she was ambulatory, they would gently rub their horns against her canes. She had trouble swallowing pills and so wrapped them in pieces of bread and swallowed those whole, the thought of which makes my throat close up. When she first went back to work full-time, she would drop a boiled and frozen chicken leg in her purse, where it would defrost by noon; that way, if somebody invited her to lunch, she could go and chuck the chicken leg without it touching her conscience. When I was a teenager, she told me that her favorite song as a teenager was "Hold Me, Thrill Me, Kiss Me," a song of such passion it mortified me to think of my young mother singing along to it on the radio. She spent hours of her life shortening clothing. She had her own tailor's standing chalk marker, with a red rubber bulb she let me operate to puff out chalk. She sometimes antagonized sports fans she knew by talking, at length, about how meaning-less and wasteful organized sports were. She hated being wrong. Once, she told a child that another word for *por-cupine* was *hedgehog*, and she did this within earshot of me and my father, and we wouldn't (I am sorry to say) let her hear the end of it. She was very often right, though not always. She was more certain of her own opinions than anybody I have ever known. She made her living for de-cades as an editor and writer at Boston University, which she was excellent at, and also as a manager of other edi-tors and writers. "The doctor told him to avoid stress at work," my mother said after my father's heart attack, "and I don't understand that. There's no stress at work. There's *excitement* at work." She loved work as much as she loved fun. Clearly she was a genius boss, helpful and forthright and fond and good-natured and memorably eccentric. Since her death I have had dozens of people—names I'd heard and plenty I hadn't—write to tell me that she was the best boss they'd ever had. One of her great delights was buying presents for her staff, individual ones that she'd thought a lot about. She might have laughed more than anyone I know. She was very funny herself. She in-sisted that she invented the mojito—I'm still unclear on her evidence—and the dark 'n' stormy, and also somehow children's Tylenol. *Simmer down, we better get a wiggle on, hold your horses.* She was a clotheshorse. She had strict rules for what she would wear, and when I shopped for presents for her, saleswomen would try to help, would display dresses and jackets, and I would have to say, *Too short, too fitted, too sheer, she'd never wear that color.* She knew by heart the entirety of Hilaire Belloc's poem "Jim, Who Ran Away from His Nurse and Was Eaten by a Lion," and I do, too, and I'm not sure whether that's because I heard her recite it so often or because I thought it was a sign of a well-rounded person. She liked to say, in conversation, "Do you know my story about . . ." and if the answer was no, she was delighted, and if it was yes, undeterred. I wish I could remember all the stories she told about herself. I can only remember the stories I remember. Which is, I suppose, all anyone ever can.

My intention had been to walk back from the theater to Trevor's. I didn't want to fight for a cab, to enter into that particular strife of strangers who all want the same thing with no method—a line, a number on a slip of paper—to fairly order them. Then I saw a bus stop, with a bus just pulling up that said *Clerkenwell Green*. I stepped upon it and swept my contactless credit card over the transponder and felt the transponder respond. A pleasure. The people who design such things know what they're doing. If it had been morning I would have climbed to the upper deck, but instead I fell into a seat near the driver and closed my eyes.

She woke me up by knocking on the glass of her booth and pointing angrily at the front door of the bus.

"Is this Clerkenwell Green?" I asked.

"It's the Clerkenwell Green stop," she said.

"You don't go to the green?"

"I'm not a taxi," she told me. "I'm a *bus*."

Trevor's was mostly dark, the street, late on a Sunday, silent and drinkerless. A boutique hotel: That meant there wasn't anyone behind the desk. Ambient light in the pocket-sized lobby, some leather armchairs. Then, out of the back, Trevor came blinking. I might have expected him in a nightcap, carrying a candle in a Wee Willie Winkie holder, but he was wearing the waistcoat and short pants.

"You all right?" he said.

"I'm all right."

"Good day?"

"I've had worse."

"Continental breakfast at eight A.M.," he said.

"My plane's at seven-thirty, alas."

"All right, darlin'," he said. "Sleep well."

I knew that once I sat at the desk in my room, I would stay awhile, peering at the internet, so I used the bathroom and washed my hands and kicked off my shoes. The whole building, whole neighborhood, felt asleep. I dialed my Texas voicemail. Six messages: four from the Russian handyman, wanting to know whether he should cut the grass; one from my mother's now-former aide, asking to borrow money; one from my mother's real estate–selling neighbor, wondering again why I hadn't engaged her to sell the house. I opened the laptop: seventy-two emails for the day, most of them junk, blue jeans on sale (I didn't wear blue jeans), pears through the mail (I only ever sent them to my parents). One from the Italian American real estate agent, saying that the house had officially been listed.

I googled my childhood address and added *for sale,* and there I was, looking at pictures of my parents' emptied house. My childhood house. The downstairs looked all right, beaten up but (I was trying to think like a stranger) like something you could reinvent. You wouldn't know, for instance, that my mother had died in the living room in a rented hospital bed, a good one, unlike the one she'd ordered from Amazon; that my father had died in his big blue recliner in the corner, drinking a beer that one of the Irish ladies had brought him. Good deaths. I hated to see them go, both of them, my cheerful mother the enthusiast, my encyclopedic and voracious and sentimental father, but from this angle especially, a quiet death in old age, people you love nearby: It feels like luck.

Look, there in the room we called the library, the last of my father's bookshelves, clinging to their Gothic principles and right angles, empty. No smell through the internet, nor the ghostly feel of dust. Revealed, all the hot-air registers that had been hidden—that one by my mother's hospital bed, this one by the TV cart. As a kid I always knew that if I was looking for some cash to buy junk food, I only had to pull up one of the cast-iron registers from the floor, and the cat hair and cobwebs underneath would have caught a dollar or more in change. I knew all the places coins collected in that house.

The bay window in the dining room was more bay-windowy than I remembered, and I lifted my head to look at the London window I was actually sitting in, like a flight deck on a TV spaceship.

The kitchen looked fine, clean, in its beige state like any bland suburban kitchen.

The front-hall stairs with their stained carpet suggested awfulness. Then the upstairs itself. For the first time in years, I could see out the second-floor windows. Neither the cleaners nor the photographer had been able to mitigate the squalor. You could tell the house had suffered, and at last I felt sorry for it. There was my old bedroom, beat to hell, the windowsill gone from one window, the mantelpiece over the sealed-up fireplace free of my childhood china bric-a-brac and bowling trophies. I was no immaculate angel. I'd left behind plenty of garbage. It was gone, too.

If I were a therapist, or a psychoanalyst, or psychologist—indeed, if I knew the difference between these things—I might work up a theory of the physical manifestation of the house. Which is that once it began to get messy, anyone outside it knowing about the mess was an invasion of privacy, and so nobody was invited in. Worse and more likely: The accumulation was a bulwark to keep people away and out. At first the house was untidy, then messy, then dirty, then a shame, a shanda, then squalid. Actual squalor. Of course my mother was embarrassed—who wouldn't be—but her exceptional powers of denial, which got her every remarkable place she went, allowed her not to dwell on it. Denial might not be just a river in Egypt, but you can travel great distances on both of them. Every now and then I would tell myself that it really *was* shameful, to be so educated, with such resources, and live in squalor. The Collyer brothers were not a picturesque story. They were a tragedy. But my parents were saved from it. They cleared out some rooms and redid the kitchen, let those rooms get dirty again, then help was in the house, and it became good enough for guests on the first floor.

My mother would hate me saying any of this. My father, too. It didn't matter how unprivate you were: If what you had to say about your life impinged on the privacy of others, then you shouldn't say it. My mother loved stories, though, particularly stories about herself, and she is, I think, the hero of this book, which she would like.

My mother was against memoir because of her belief in privacy. How could you not want to guard it, she thought, she who as a child was in and out of hospitals, in and out of surgery, had to fight for every bit of privacy and autonomy she had. She believed in privacy the way some people believe in modesty: a virtue for everyone. Only when in private, my mother thought—I *think* she thought—could you defy expectations. Imagine what you can accomplish when strangers and parents and doctors and children leave you alone! It's good for you, intensely pleasurable, to have things you think about yourself that you don't reveal to other people. Things you hide in your fiction without claiming as your own. Even your particular self-loathings are dear and useful. Enlivening. It's called, my mother might have said, an inner life: the one thing nobody can take away from you.

Once, I would have said that I knew everything about my mother, even what she didn't tell me, the peculiarities of her ego and her sense of humor, her favorite jokes, her cocktail order, the color and heft of a scarf that would delight her, the sort of novel she'd both admire and want to argue with, exactly how to help her stand up from a chair, help her into a car or bed. I was wrong. I only knew the stories she liked to tell, not the ones she'd prefer to forget. When I lifted her foot onto a step with my foot— the Footjack—and it was what my mother would call a particularly or mysteriously stiff day, I knew what my leg felt like, not hers.

When I write, I think, *That's wrong, but I'll get it right later on.* Eventually I think, *That's wrong, but I'll get it right in the next book.* For everything wrong in this book, I apologize: I meant to fix it. I will fix it.

We're not our souls, we're not our bodies; we're the shimmering border between.

All this history going on without my mother in it. What would she have thought? My mother's life was one of history: child of the Depression, of World War II, of the polio epidemic, of the women's liberation movement, of the civil rights movement. She wasn't special. Everyone exists in history. How strange that we have passed from one era into a different one since her death. I am not being poetic: Everything is different not because she is dead, though that would have sufficed, but because it is 2022 and everything is different.

The dead have no privacy left, is what I've decided. Somebody else might decide otherwise, that the only thing the dead have left is privacy. Anyhow, here in this book, I am writing about the dead and the fictional, and not the living and the actual, whom I love, and whom I will leave alone.

Or else I'm just so self-centered that I don't want to consider anybody else's feelings. Especially my mother's. My beloved mother's. How awful and incredible, to not worry about her feelings—though I do, of course; my hands are trembling as I type this. *But it's my story, too,* I might tell her, *even if you are the hero of it.* There are plenty of secrets I haven't told.

Why are you writing about me?

Because otherwise you'd evanesce, and that I cannot bear.

Me, evanesce? Not one of my talents.